She did and didn't want to be there.

Time had slipped away, as if there had never been anyone else holding her. As if she had been the only one for him. They were eighteen again and in love. They'd been each other's first love. That had been such a magical time.

Theda moved away as Hunter tried to kiss her. She didn't want him to kiss her because she didn't want to go back to what they'd been those long years ago. She couldn't go to that place again.

"Why didn't you tell me you were moving here?" she asked.

"I was afraid you'd tell me not to come," he said after a long pause. "Would you have told me to come?"

"I don't know. Probably. You hurt me…."

"I tried to explain," he said.

"Yes, you did, but eighteen-year-olds aren't very good at understanding things. We could have clung to each other and made it through everything."

"I feel that now, but hindsight isn't worth a damn," he said roughly.

Books by Francine Craft

Kimani Romance

If Love Is Good to Me
Never Without You…Again

Kimani Arabesque

Devoted
The Black Pearl
A Mother's Love
Lyrics of Love
Still in Love
Wedding Bells
Star Crossed
Betrayed by Love
Forever Love
Love in Bloom
What Matters Most
Haunted Heart
Born to Love You
Give Love
The Best of Everthing
Wild Heart
Dreams of Ecstasy
Passion's Fool

FRANCINE CRAFT

is the pen name of a Washington, D.C.-based writer who has enjoyed writing for many years. A native Mississippian, she has been a research assistant for a large psychological organization, an elementary school teacher, a business-school instructor and a federal-government legal secretary. Francine's hobbies include reading, photography and songwriting. She deeply cherishes time spent with her good friends.

Never Without *You*... *Again*

FRANCINE CRAFT

KIMANI™
ROMANCE

KIMANI PRESS™

ISBN-13: 978-0-373-86037-1
ISBN-10:   0-373-86037-4

NEVER WITHOUT YOU...AGAIN

Copyright © 2007 by Francine Craft

www.kimanipress.com

Printed in U.S.A.

Dear Reader,

The story of Hunter Davis and Theda Coles has been in my head for a long time. Photography is one of my hobbies and, as I am with most of the arts, I can go into orbit thinking about it. Hunter and Theda were young, ill-fated lovers who found each other again in their thirties, both having married and lost others. But they were also fated to marry, and this story tells how that comes about.

What happens to Theda as she seeks to become principal of a high school is a story of what can happen when human wretchedness shows its ugly head. Hunter's evil ex-wife will stop at nothing to get him back. She uses compromising fake photos to discredit Theda and upset the whole community. She tries to ruin Theda's career and end her relationship with Hunter, but her scheming backfires. Her efforts just bring Hunter and Theda closer together, and nothing will stop them now.

With love and best wishes,

Francine

Dedication

To Duane Kevin Woodard (D.K.), one of the most talented, engaging and just altogether wonderful young men I have known. The son of my dear friend, Saundra, he is slated to continue making this world a richer and more joyous place.

Vivian Fitz Roy—a precious and treasured friend who cannot go out of this world before I do.

Acknowledgment

I acknowledge my debt to God and to so many people who have helped me greatly. Most of the time, people are more wonderful than we give them credit for being.

Chapter 1

Theda Coles hurried along the corridor of Crystal Lake, Virginia's Harney High. It was registration day and laughing groups of students stood about. Racing to the principal's office for what seemed like the millionth time that day, she slammed smack into a tall male figure. She looked up into his face and for a moment her heart flipped crazily and she couldn't breathe.

"Hunter," she said in a hoarse whisper.

The tall, ruddy-skinned man was having trouble breathing, too, as his arms went around her. He said only, "Theda."

They stood staring at one another for long moments. He regained some semblance of composure first. A few of the students had stopped the conversation to gawk and giggle. One drawled, "Hey, get a room!"

Drawing a deep breath while steadying her, Hunter Davis smiled. The change in his expression caused Harney High's usually unflappable guidance counselor's mind to spin.

"I've moved here and I brought my son to register. I called, but your answering service said you were away," he said.

"Yes. I just got back in town this morning. How *are* you?"

"I could tell you more about how I am and find out about you if you'd have lunch with me. I need to talk with you alone. Can you get away?"

She shook her head. "I'm afraid not," she said as she glanced at the bunches of students loitering in the hallway.

"We need to talk. There's so much to be said."

She nodded. "What about dinner? I could meet you at a restaurant called Marshall's outside of town? I could give you directions. Where are you staying?"

"I'm moving into the old Turner house."

Theda grimaced inside. The imposing Turner house was next door to Keatha Ames, a highly vocal school board member and one of her archenemies. She wished her heart would stop drumming. But looking at the man she had once loved more than life wouldn't let her heart quit its happy thumping. Her silly knees were shaking. He had been a handsome youth. Now he was a drop-dead gorgeous man.

Hunter's heart was doing its own dance. Damn, she looked good. Her oval face was still warm and entrancing. She had tinted her hair dark auburn and her golden-brown eyes still sparkled in her cinnamon-colored face. Looking at her lush figure, he salivated with memory. Images of her naked in his arms flashed through his mind. Tender moments, too. Times when they had simply held each other and dreamed of their future. Then came the pain of separation he hated remembering.

"Why don't you let me pick you up since you know the way," he asked.

She told him her address then and he nodded. "You know I'll be there. What time?"

She hesitated only a moment, smiling. "How about six o'clock? Too early?"

"Not early enough, but it will have to do."

Neither wanted to leave, but she had a principal waiting for her and he had to get his son registered.

A security guard paused and smiled at them as they lingered in the corridor.

Angela Smith, Theda's best friend, passed them, smiling brightly, and Theda stopped the other woman and introduced her to Hunter.

"Um-m-m," the flirtatious Angela said. "So I meet the fabulously famous photographer, Hunter Davis. Your book on South Africa, *Change Out of Chaos,* is a bestseller. Congratulations!"

Hunter's deep baritone conveyed his pleasure. "It came from deep inside my heart. I'm glad you liked it."

Angela was an art teacher and everything in the field fascinated her. A medium tall, chocolate-skinned, dark-haired woman, she also dabbled in photography. Theda saw the appreciative gleam in her friend's gaze as Angela gave Hunter the once-over with her eyes.

As Angela moved away, Theda murmured, "I really have to go."

"I know, and I hate that you do. But I'll see you at six." On impulse he leaned forward and kissed her cheek and she thought she'd lose it. Hot tears lay just behind her eyelids. This man had hurt her terribly, had hurt her as much as he'd loved her, and here she was mooning over him as though they were both eighteen years old again.

They'd had quite a history together, but it had been over a long time ago. He was married now, with a son. Tonight they'd talk about his family and her widowhood. That surely was nothing to get excited about. *You're a fool,* she told her heart as she hurried to the principal's office.

Going into the office of Andre Lord, the principal, she closed the door and leaned against it, her knees still shaking.

"Well, you look all shook up," he said as he looked up from the reports he had been reading.

She calmed then. Andre was a sweetheart. Only forty-two, he was a handsome man with reddish brown hair and a well-toned body. Steady, dependable, he had long ago declared himself in love with her. He'd even offered marriage, but after two heartbreaks, Theda had vowed never to love or to accept a man's love again.

Theda walked to the window and looked out. The late-August sun was high and the day was beautiful with a cerulean sky blessing them.

Turning back to Andre, she smiled as he put his head to one side, "What *is* there about you today, Theda?" He got up and went to stand beside her. "I know we've got business to talk about, but first things first. What's up? You know Reverend Whisonant and I are doing everything we can to see that you replace me when I go on sabbatical next year. Have you heard something?"

She shook her head. "You'll know before I do. No, I…" She stopped. Talking about Hunter was too personal.

"I'll tell you sometime," she said. "But for now, why did you want to see me?"

Out in the corridor again, Hunter and a lanky dark brown youth stood near Andre's office. She almost laughed because she would know the boy anywhere. He was a teenage version of Hunter's father. His hair was black and curly and he had Hunter's black eyes. Glancing from son to father, she drank in Hunter's Cherokee red skin, soot-black hair and his six-foot-two wonderfully fit body.

It was only a few seconds, but it seemed much longer before he introduced the boy. Courteous to a fault, Curt Davis took her hand and held it a moment. "You're as pretty as my father said you were," he told her. "I'm told I'm kinda wild. I'll probably land in your office more than once. In the meantime, I'm angling for a motorcycle like Dad's. Could you help me persuade him?"

Theda laughed. "You don't ask for much."

"I'm a senior and he still thinks of me as a kid. I'll be seventeen soon."

One year younger than she and Hunter had been when their affair had taken off. Why in hell did she keep thinking about that? Didn't her heart know the meaning of something being *over.*

Kitty Sanders, a senior, walked by then and Theda stopped her and introduced Hunter and Curt.

"Oh, we've met," Kitty said. "I took them under my wing and showed them around a bit." She and Curt looked at each other flirtatiously. "Curt's into photography and so am I. And Mr. Davis is famous. This is my lucky day. Curt, why don't I take you to see the cafeteria and give your dad and Dr. Coles a chance to talk?"

The boy and Kitty walked away. "Would you

like to see my office?" How formal she sounded. As if she had never lain naked in his arms.

"I wish I had the time. But I'm late for a meeting and I've got so much settling in to do. Can I have a raincheck?" He glanced at his watch. He appeared reluctant to go.

He seemed to be flirting with her, Theda thought. He wasn't wearing a wedding ring. Were he and his wife separated? Divorced? No, sophisticated men in the world he lived in had dinner with other women, old flames, without their wives and went home and discussed the meal and conversation.

"I knew when your husband died," he said suddenly. "I sent condolences." Yes, she remembered that. Her heart had hurt with double pain.

She had to ask it. "Has your wife come yet?"

His voice sounded harsh, brusque. "My *ex*-wife. We've been divorced for over two years." He didn't tell her how much he had wanted to look her up when he'd been suffering so over the blows his ex had dealt him. Theda had always been able to soothe his pain.

He was free. Theda tried to calm herself. *You never learn, do you?* Hurt is something she seemed to keep asking for. He'd told her many,

many years ago it wouldn't work between them. What made her think anything had changed?

"I really do have to go now. I've got a load of paperwork and I need to get ready for my next student appointments. I'll see you tonight."

"All right," he said, and left.

Back in her big office, she lifted her hands over her head and contemplated her muddled feelings.

Angela came in, grinning, with eyes half-closed. "Well, well, well…" she said.

"He's divorced, but he was single back when he cut me loose. Things won't be any different this time. But I agreed to see him tonight. He's picking me up for dinner."

Angela raised her eyebrows. "Seems to me, girlfriend, like you guys are picking up right where you left off. Oops, gotta run. It seems to me I've got a zillion new students. And just for the record, your man is to die for. I wish *I* had me one of him."

Theda shook her head. "He's not my man."

"Whatever you say, but call me when you get home, *if* you get home tonight."

"Oh, I'll get home, all right. Fool me once, shame on you, fool me twice—"

"I'd be willing to be a fool for the likes of

Hunter Davis. And he comes complete with a cutie son...."

Theda smiled because Angela was very happily married and the mother of three.

As if Angela had called him, Curt and Kitty came into the room. Angela left and the two teenagers stood in front of Theda's desk smiling broadly. "We're going to register in just a few minutes, but I wanted to talk with you a bit. You know I'm into photography these days and Curt says he'll help me. Isn't that great?"

"It surely is. Curt, we're so happy to have you with us. Sorry you needed to transfer in your senior year, but we'll do everything we can to make it worth your while."

Curt smiled. "Yeah, I was sorry, too, until I met Kitty. Now somehow it doesn't seem bad."

Like father, like son, Theda thought. Charmers, both of them.

Chapter 2

At home late that afternoon, Theda didn't know how she'd gotten through the day after Hunter left. Kitty and Curt had come back for a while, looking pleased with themselves. Theda was glad Kitty had found a friend and Curt was a peach. He reminded her of her late son, Kelly, and thinking of Kelly and her late husband, Art, still hurt too much.

As she showered and dressed for her date that night with Hunter, she couldn't help thinking about how their relationship had ended years before. He'd sent her a letter saying their relationship had to be over.

She told herself not to focus on that now. But it was hard not to. She was so lonely.

Hunter had set her very soul on fire. Then he had left her. Art had come along and he had loved her gently and well. There hadn't been the aching passion she'd known with Hunter, but she and Art had enjoyed a soft, tender, satisfying love. It had torn her heart for the second time when he'd died.

She went to her walk-in closet and shifted dresses around. What should she wear, she wondered. It seemed to take her too long to settle on a dark navy silk dress. The style of the expensive dress complimented her curves and the color went well with her copper skin. She decided on strappy sandals that flattered her long legs, and she chose pearl earrings as her only jewelry.

Lord, she was nervous. All afternoon she had dropped things, made mistakes. Now she sat on the edge of the bed and did deep breathing exercises, but when she stood up, she was still shaking. Why was she trying so hard, she asked herself. *Why hadn't he let her know he was moving to Crystal Lake?* A bit of anger replaced her nervousness. He hadn't cared enough then and he didn't care enough now, she thought. Hunter had a lot of questions to answer.

He came a little early, and she was glad to see he was nervous, too. Anger forgotten, she came close to salivating when he showed up, looking as fine as ever in a black suit with shirt and a tie. Hunter inherited his sun-kissed coloring from his Cherokee mother and his handsome features from his African-American father. His black eyes were smoldering as he looked at her. She invited him in, but evaded his attempt to kiss her.

He whistled then, long and low and she flushed hotly. "You're still fresh, I see," she said drily. Only then did she notice the small, square florist's box in his hand. It was pathetic how he could still mesmerize her.

He held the box out. "For you. In memory of what once was and could be again."

How could he? He was the one who'd walked away.

His voice was husky. "I want to kiss you so badly, but you turn away."

He wasn't making it easy for her. She took the clear plastic box in which nestled one of the most beautiful white orchids she'd ever seen. He'd given her an orchid once before when she was in college. No special occasion. "Orchids are like you," he'd said, "precious."

She went to the full-length mirror and pinned on the orchid. He used to pin them on, but she didn't want him that close to her.

"You're very angry and I don't blame you," he said, "but I'm angry with you, too. Let's go so we can talk this out, salvage what we can. It's plain to me we still belong together."

It was early for dinner at Marshall's and the restaurant was half empty. Among the early diners were Reverend Wiley Whisonant and his wife. Theda led Hunter over and introduced him to the older couple. Mrs. Whisonant smiled and raised her eyebrows at Theda. Reverend Whisonant pumped Hunter's hand enthusiastically.

"As you can see," the reverend joked, "we left the rest of the family home tonight. We put a little extra romance into our lives as often as we can." They had six boys.

Mrs. Whisonant flushed, lowering her eyes. The Whisonants were two of Theda's favorite people. Theda was active in the church. The older couple bade Theda and Hunter a good dinner as Rick Marshall, the restaurant's owner, led them

over to a front corner table. The spot overlooked
the spacious grounds featuring a big domed fish-
pond and huge goldfish of all colors. The setting
sun offered a splendid view.

Sipping the sparkling water and nibbling on
oyster crackers at their table, Theda felt her nervousness return.

Hunter looked at Theda intently, caressing,
kissing her with his gaze.

"So we're angry with each other," he said. "I
want to explain my part and I want to hear yours.
I still love you, baby. I'm not going to beat around
the bush about that."

When she didn't respond he plunged on.

"I'm going to dive right in with my part. You
know I left in the middle of our sophomore year at
Howard. My dad got transferred to Texarkana to
work on the army base there. A plum job he couldn't
pass up. You and I had plans to marry early, but both
of our families felt we were too young. They wisely
realized how in love we were. But then my dad had
a sudden, massive heart attack that killed him in-
stantly. I wrote you and you sent me the most beautiful condolence telegram of all. I called and you
soothed me, wanted to come down, but I couldn't
let you." She relived that time as he talked.

"Mom went to pieces before Dad was cold." He paused a long moment. "It was only a few days after the funeral when we found that my dad owed a mountain of debts, many of which we couldn't pay with what was left of his estate."

She placed her slender hand over his. "I'm so sorry. I didn't know. I would have come."

"I know. And I knew, too, you would have come. Mom had to be hospitalized and there were additional expenses. A public facility would have killed her, so I put her in a private, very expensive place, but she wasn't improving. Her life seemed to be over."

His breath came fast then before he spoke. "I wrote you that very long letter, telling you it had to be over between us...." He paused a long moment. "You always had goals. You wanted to be married, but you also intended to be a high school principal. You glowed when you talked of getting your doctorate and making a difference in some high school."

Theda felt her anger slipping away. "I would have come to you."

He nodded. "I know you would have, but I couldn't let you. Dad had made me promise to always take care of my mother. I took three jobs, but it wasn't enough. Then Brad Ware, a wealthy man who owns a chain of photography studios across the country, hired me as a photographer and took me under his wing. He had no sons and wanted one. He was really good to me. He had a daughter who had a crush on me.

"I finally had to file for bankruptcy and he got his high-powered lawyer to handle it. I thought I saw a way out and I started back to Crystal Lake to surprise you, ask you to marry me at last." He was silent, remembering. "Twenty miles out from the city I picked up a Crystal Lake paper and leafed through it thinking of you. Your photo was on the front page of the society section. You had married Art Coles....

"I went back to Texas without calling you. God, I was bitter. Brad's daughter had a crush on me and I caved in to that crush. I couldn't take the pain I was feeling and so out of desperation I began to date her. We married a short while later. At eighteen, I had a wife, not the wife of my dreams, but a wife. When I was nineteen Curt was born and my mom died of cancer. I'll talk about the rest later, but I need to know what you're thinking—what you're feeling."

She cleared her throat and bit her bottom lip. "Do you have a photo of your ex-wife?"

He shook his head. "Not any longer. Why don't you show me a photo of Art." He was somehow certain she carried a photo and he was a little jealous. He had remembered Art's name all these years.

Her heart hurt for her late husband and son, yet she was thrilled to be this close to Hunter. Theda got her purse from the floor and dug into it. With trembling fingers, she slipped the photo from its slot in her wallet and handed it to him. A photo of Art, Kelly and her with their arms around each other. They'd spent a wonderful weekend in New York, seeing a Broadway show and sightseeing. They had been in front of the Metropolitan Museum of Art.

Looking at the photo, Hunter felt the breath knocked out of him. "The kid looks like…" he began. Then he stared at her in agony. "He's *my* kid, isn't he?"

She nodded as scalding tears filled his eyes.

"*Was* yours. He and Art died together in the plane crash. Ten others and I were the only survivors."

Shocked speechless, he sat silent for a few minutes. At last he said, "I'm so sorry. What can I say that would make any difference? I should have been with you when you were carrying him." His voice was half-strangled. "I want to go somewhere and hold you the way I should have held you then and when they died. I don't feel like eating. Can we go somewhere?"

She nodded. He beckoned to Marshall, told him something had come up and paid for the uneaten meal. Marshall was sympathetic. "Come again," he said.

"We will," they both said.

In Hunter's burgundy sports car, they drove to the waterfront and he parked along the tree-lined boardwalk and took her in his arms.

She did and didn't want to be there. Time had slipped away as if there had never been anyone else holding her. They were eighteen again. First loves for each other. It had been magic making Kelly. She had been devastated when Hunter had abandoned her and she'd been desperate. But Art had helped her through it. He'd loved her, married her and then Art and Kelly had died. She pressed herself into Hunter's hard, muscular body, desperately seeking comfort. He stroked her back wordlessly and kissed her face.

She didn't want him to kiss her because she

wasn't going back to that place again. After a very long time, she sat up, sighing, and asked him, "Why didn't you tell me you were moving here?"

He thought about it a long moment. "I was afraid you'd tell me not to come, so like the proverbial bull in the china shop, I came blundering in. A real-estate broker I know lived for a while in Crystal Lake, so she knew about the house. I bought it without even seeing it. I trust her. Would you have told me not to come?"

"I don't know. Probably. You hurt me...."

"Forgive me. I tried to explain."

"Yes, you did, but eighteen-year-olds aren't very good at understanding things. We might have made it if we had stayed together."

"I feel that now, but hindsight is often not worth a damn. How long have Art and my son been dead?"

"Two years in October. And he was more Art's son than yours."

"He's the spitting image of me."

"Yes, and in the beginning I was angry with him for looking so much like you, but he was such a lovable, appealing baby," she said with a sad laugh. "Does it ever stop hurting?"

He reached over and pulled her to him again. "I want to do everything I can to make it stop hurting. I want to start again with you, angel face, if you'll just forgive me and let me."

"You always called me angel face," she said. "And I called you A.G. for African god."

"You spoiled me. I thought I owned the earth then. I thought *we* owned the earth. You were my goddess. You still are."

Wanting to be rid of a little of the pain, she said, "Tell me about your wife. Are you still in love with her?"

He shook his head. "Not anymore. It's been over two years since she told me she wanted a divorce. She married an oil baron who can give her the world, she told me. She left Curt and me without a backward glance."

"You sound a little bitter. Is she beautiful?"

"I thought so until I remembered you." He hesitated a long moment. "Some people come into our lives like a meteor and they knock us off our feet. That was Helena. Others are steady, shining stars and they last forever. Theda, I had to come to you. You know I would have come to you after the crash if I had known."

"I know. Just as I would have come to you

had I known about your father's debt and your mother's illness. Life is funny. It throws us for a loop sometimes."

He smoothed her hair. "Will you take me to Kelly's and Art's grave?"

"Yes. They're buried in Art's family's cemetery."

"I knew Art was in love with you when I met him. I'm glad he married you. As glad as I can be that you married anybody else."

She drew a deep breath. "Hunter, we can go to the cemetery tonight. I know the caretaker well. I used to go there at night when I couldn't sleep."

"I'd like that."

At the beautiful, small cemetery they stood looking at the two graves and Hunter held her hand tightly as they both cried.

The night was overcast now as they walked back to the car, both silent and sick with memory.

Back in the car, Hunter leaned toward her, his voice urgent. "Honey, let's not waste any more time. Let's get married right away. God knows, we blazed a very romantic path when we were younger."

She shook her head no. "I want to go very, very slow. I hurt so much for so long. My every nerve is sensitive to you, Hunter, the way I've never been to anyone else, but I'm not sure I can take any more hurt. Perhaps we could just be friends."

Hunter felt his heart plunge, but he knew where she was coming from. And yet, he wasn't a man who gave up easily. He'd always fought for what he wanted and he intended to fight for her now. Yeah, he'd go as slow as she wanted, but in the end he intended to have her.

He nuzzled her a bit as the old familiar thrills shot through him, but she drew away. The old, familiar thrills felt the way nothing else had ever felt.

"Okay," he finally said, "we'll take it slow the way you want to. Lord knows I owe you that. Just let me be with you. I think you know how much I love you, how much we love each other."

She stirred a bit. "Hunter, let's go in."

To her surprise he didn't argue. "Okay, but I've got an idea. I know tomorrow's a workday for you, but I'd love for you to help me settle in. Please."

"Okay, but not for too long. It'll give me a chance to see Curt again. You've raised yourself a great kid."

He sighed then. "I didn't have too much to do with it. Well, maybe I did. Curt's spent a lot of time with his great-grandfather, my mother's father. He's really into his Native American heritage. He would rather sleep under a teepee than indoors any time. He can roll thunder drums and he knows Indian lore like the back of his hand. Any kudos belong to Gray Wolf."

They were silent before she told him, "Let's go."

In a short while they pulled into Hunter's driveway. Floodlights were on in back, and Curt was shooting baskets with a vengeance. They joined him.

"Hello, Dr. Coles. Glad you came by. Gives me a chance to show off."

"Let me see you strut your stuff," she said.

Laughing, Curt stood near center court and made a couple of difficult baskets as Theda called "Bravo!"

"He's also a hotdog," his father said, throwing off his coat onto a nearby chair and joining his son.

In a few minutes, Theda saw where Curt's talent came from. Hunter dribbled the ball and sprang into the air near the basket, dunked it expertly, dribbled and dunked it again.

"Okay, guys, get ready for some *real* action," she called. Art had been a master at anything athletic and he'd taught her well. But she hadn't played since he died.

Now Theda kicked off her sandals and signaled for the ball. Their mouths hung open with surprise. She dribbled several feet from the basket and then made a jump shot.

"Hey, Mama," Curt chortled, "you're good! You can shoot hoops with me any old time. You tell me your hoop dreams and I'll tell you mine."

After a moment, Hunter told her, "Got something to show you."

As Curt continued making baskets, Hunter led her to the garage. He threw the black covers off and there stood a gleaming new Harley-Davidson motorcycle.

"Like her?" He was grinning like a teenager.

"Beautiful, yes, but I never approved of your riding motorcycles."

"I know, but like you, they're in my blood."

His mouth went down at the corners as he teased her. "Want to go for a spin?"

"Not on your life," she snorted.

He came closer and she inhaled his cologne and sweat.

"You used to ride behind me, holding on to me, even if you were afraid."

"I grew up," she said coolly.

His eyes devoured her body. "Yeah, you sure did. Later maybe."

"Don't count on it."

They went back to Curt then and simply watched him shoot.

A woman's throat cleared behind them and a thin, reedy voice called out, "Anybody home?" Keatha Ames, Hunter's next-door neighbor strode onto the court. "Well, I don't play such a good game, but I heard voices and thought I'd join in." In her sixties, Keatha was short and stocky with dyed black hair and pale yellow skin.

Both males greeted the older woman warmly, but Theda was not as friendly. Keatha's son, who now worked overseas with the State Department, had fallen hard for Theda after Art's death and Keatha thought they'd be a good match. But Theda hadn't been attracted to Mort, and Keatha had taken it harder than he had. Now Keatha was doing her best to be charming to the two males and cold to Theda.

"You've been here three days and I haven't re-ally seen your house," Keatha said. "Tomorrow

I'm making tuna casserole, one for you two and one for me. It's got peas, onion, carrots. You won't have to cook." She looked at Hunter wistfully. "I only saw a little of your house the other day. Why don't you show me around a bit."

She didn't remark on the fact that Hunter had company.

"Well," Hunter said slowly, "I have plans…"

Theda felt as though she had been in a daze. Here she was in one of her best dresses shooting hoops in a backyard. *Had she lost her mind?* Very quickly she said, "Tomorrow's still a rough day for me and I have to get home."

Keatha couldn't have been more delighted. There was only Hunter's car and Curt's old Ford Mustang in the driveway. That meant Hunter would be taking Miss High and Mighty home.

"You go right ahead," Keatha said to Hunter. "I'll be right here when you get back. If Curt has to go to bed, I'll just sit quietly and wait."

Out on the highway as the Porsche motor purred quietly, Hunter glanced at her. "You sure didn't stay long. Did Mrs. Ames chase you away? There doesn't seem to be any love lost between you two."

Theda smiled a little. "I'll go into it later. And, Hunter, thanks for backing off. I really appreciate it."

"Sure," was all he said.

Later he insisted on seeing her in. "Let me come in for just a moment," he said.

Inside he checked out her house, complimented her on the well-appointed, modern decor and her security system. Then when they stood by the front door, he took her in his arms with a gentle movement. He held her, simply held her as her body threatened to explode with passion. She shouldn't have let him come in, she thought.

For the life of her she couldn't ask him not to kiss her. She wanted it too much, as she felt him stroke her back and nuzzle her throat. Then he tore himself away asking, "Could we try to actually eat dinner at Marshall's tomorrow night?"

She hesitated a moment. "I shouldn't see you too often."

"After tomorrow night, I'll promise not to be greedy."

"Thank you. I've received two body blows in my life. Your leaving me and Art's and Kelly's death. I don't know if I could ever go back to the way it was between us."

"I've told you how sorry I am I deserted you. Believe me, I suffered, too. I used to come awake at night wanting you so badly I wanted to die. All those years, my love, I was never without you. I've told you before and I'll say it again. You can heal with time, but you have to try."

"I'm just so open to you. You can hurt me with a glance."

"I'll never hurt you again, angel face. I'm going to spend the rest of my life making this up to you."

Chapter 3

"**I**'m not looking forward to the meeting this morning." Theda closed her eyes as she and Angela sat in her office drinking cups of coffee.

Angela looked at her friend. Theda looked a little sleepy, but since the first day of school she had been full of life. Hunter Davis had to be the cause. "The meeting's with Reverend Whisonant, Andre and—" here Angela lifted her eyebrows and laughed a little "—the witch of Crystal Lake, Keatha Ames."

"Angela, I want this so much. Andre praises my

ideas all the time and I feel I can do great things. Filling in for him will do so much to prepare me to take over a school of my own. Wish me luck."

Angela smiled. "You don't need luck, love. You've got it all. Andre and Reverend Whisonant mean something in this town. I know Keatha's a powerhouse with her money and her sharp tongue, but this time I'm betting she loses. Do you ever hear from Mort, Keatha's son?"

"No, and I don't want to. He was just as nasty as his mother when he learned I wasn't interested in him."

Angela grimaced as she drained the last of her black coffee, patting her short, curly Afro that flattered her dark bronze skin. Angela was medium height and athletic. She and Theda had been friends since childhood. "Let's talk about something fun. How's it going with Hunter?"

Theda blushed and her body got warm. "He called last night and I said I couldn't talk long, but I did most of the talking and it was after midnight when we stopped. We talked about my future in the school system. I'd almost forgotten what a terrific listener he is."

"You're seeing him a lot, aren't you?"

"Not really. He took me to dinner that first

night and we were both so...overcome. We talked about how we broke up when we were eighteen and we talked about Art and Kelly."

"I'm glad. You needed to talk. I'm your friend, but you were holding back. Hunter's really good for you, Theda."

"I don't want to be hurt again." She thought she was beginning to sound like a broken record. No one wanted to be hurt, but it went with life and living.

"Hunter called again this morning before I left the house. He asked me to go with him to visit a jeweler friend of his to look at cufflinks for Curt. He wants to give them to Curt for his birthday. I told him I'd be too busy today, but I want to get something special for Curt, too. You don't turn seventeen every day."

Angela pursed her lips. "You don't fall in love again every day, either."

Theda was very still. "We'll see. This time I'm insisting that we go like molasses in the January cold. Last time we raced ahead and look what happened."

Angela got up and came to Theda, bent and stroked her shoulder. "The man loves you. His heart is in his eyes when he looks at you. Be kind to him."

Angela left and Theda got up, began to rummage about in her desk, collecting the files and papers she wanted to take to her meeting. Funny how she could still hear Hunter's voice caressing her ears. Drifting to sleep the night before, she had been tormented with visions of being in his arms and in love all those years ago.

She shuddered and ruthlessly cut off those memories. She had a life to live and she wasn't certain she wanted Hunter to be part of it.

Once in Andre's office, Theda did her best to relax. "I'm not usually this nervous," she told him. "But I can't seem to settle down."

They sat at a small conference table in the cramped office. Theda could feel Andre's gaze assessing her.

"I saw you and Hunter the other night at Marshall's," he said. "I started to come over, but I didn't want to horn in." He hesitated a moment. "You two were having a serious conversation."

"You're always welcome to horn in on any conversation I have," Theda said.

He drew a deep breath, wanting to disagree with her. They had looked so intimate sitting there he knew they would not appreciate an interruption. He also knew enough of Hunter's and her story to know he would always lose to Hunter when it came to winning Theda's heart.

Just then Reverend Whisonant arrived. His larger-than-life personality filled the room. It was still a little early. The meeting was to begin at ten. "Morning, folks. You all look ready for just about anything, and with Mrs. Ames just about anything is possible," he said with a chuckle.

Reverend Whisonant was not a man to mince words. He was a gentle man, but he was also outspoken. As he sat down, he said, "This is going to be a big year for you, lady. And I'm going to do everything I can to back Dr. Coles to the hilt."

"Thank you," Theda told him.

Andre looked thoughtful. "Come November, I'll be training her to take over. I'm hiring a new guidance counselor and Dr. Coles will be co-principal with me." He stroked the side of his nose. "Now, there's something wrong with that sentence structure, but you get the idea."

Reverend Whisonant laughed. "No problem." He turned to Theda. "I want to hear a whole lot more about your plans for placing senior students in internships in businesses here in Crystal Lake. Have you finalized things yet?"

She shook her head. "I hope to have something soon. It's a concept that's being tried all over the country and it's working well. The students are *very* enthusiastic about the idea."

"And they should be," Reverend Whisonant said. He asked more questions then and she answered gravely, bringing a pleased expression to his face. "I've got two of my kids here at Harney, so I'm invested in the school's success. In addition, many of my flock have kids here. I guess you could say I couldn't be more vested."

At a quarter after ten, Andre looked at his watch. It was to be a short meeting and Keatha still wasn't here. Well, he thought, she had a reputation for running late. He had once read in a psychological journal that people who were constantly late were often hostile. That certainly fit Keatha Ames.

"I had other fish to fry, I'm telling you." Keatha came into the office breathlessly, clutching her black designer purse and a tote. She didn't apologize for being late. She considered it her due. "No need to catch me up. I can imagine what was being said."

Andre filled her in anyway. Her eyes were cold and hard when he finished.

"I'm sure *you* think it's a good idea," she said,

regarding Reverend Whisonant with a snide expression on her face.

"I certainly do. One of the best I've heard in ages. It's something we should have done years ago."

Keatha stroked her face with elegantly wrinkled hands. Her beautifully manicured nails were painted a bright red. "I don't mind saying I think this is a foolish idea," she snorted. "I'm for focusing on the three *R*'s. Our kids aren't well trained and there's a world of time for them to get into the workplace. Let's focus on the essentials, I say."

They were all silent for a few minutes, then Reverend Whisonant spoke up. "I don't think you're going over this carefully enough. We have a lot of poor and nearly poor kids in Crystal Lake. They'll need to go to work as soon as possible and this plan will be very helpful..."

"Well, I for one, don't think the school should be catering to its poorest element. The rest of us need consideration, too. I'm not ashamed of being rich. Let them come up to me. I'm not going down to them," Keatha said.

Theda shook her head. "We need to help the less fortunate," she began.

"Well, what else do we have to talk about?"

Keatha demanded. "I tell you I'm going to fight this silly plan and I don't mind telling you I'm going to fight not to have you take Andre's place, as well. I think your ideas are just too wild-eyed."

"No," Andre said gently. "They're really good ideas. We need to do everything we can to help our youth. Too many are dropping out. They're disinterested. We're not holding their attention."

Keatha raised her eyebrows as high as they would go and her pale skin had reddened considerably.

"My son went to Harney High, finished with honors and went on to Howard where he graduated with honors. Not everyone appreciates him…" She shot a malevolent glance at Theda. "He's a wonderful man and he's very successful. I'll bet you his Spanish wife appreciates him."

Both Andre and Reverend Whisonant had trouble keeping a straight face. Neither had forgotten how ardently Mort Ames had pursued Theda and how badly he and his mother had taken it when she'd turned him down.

As the meeting drew to a close, they talked of other school matters. At no point in the conversation did Keatha agree with any of them.

"Got me a nice new neighbor," Keatha broke

in suddenly. "Reminds me of Mort. Nice teenage boy, too. I'm going to work on Hunter. He'll be interested in what his son's doing at school."

Theda noted that the older woman's face had lit up, grown softer. Theda thought, oh, what a man could do for you.

The meeting broke up a short while later. Keatha left saying, "I'm going to fight this and you, missy." She pointed a finger at Theda. "Got your master's and your doctorate at Columbia. New York City. Well, we don't need sin city's ways down here. What's right for New York isn't right for Crystal Lake," she said.

Theda thought she'd change the subject. "One thing we haven't talked about is the Christmas dance. This year it's at the gorgeous Masonic Lodge and the whole community is taking part."

"Lots of riffraff that way," Keatha scoffed.

"I prefer to think of it as lots of nice people who deserve to be included," Reverend Whisonant said. "It's going to cost more, of course, but it will be worth it in terms of goodwill."

"When my son was here, the Christmas party was confined to Harney and I'm sure that was best," Keatha said.

Oh, yes, Theda thought, anything closed and

exclusive was to Keatha's liking. If, as the Bible stated, "the last would be first," Keatha was going to be out of luck.

"Well, there's plenty of time to thrash this out," Reverend Whisonant said. "I get the feeling we're going to have a great party."

"We'll probably need D.C. cops, as well as our own," Keatha snorted.

The other three people smiled and Andre said, "Let's look on the bright side."

Reverend Whisonant and Keatha left together as if they were the best of friends. "I'll see you in church Sunday," the reverend said to Theda and she nodded. She didn't go to church often since her family's passing, but she intensely enjoyed it when she did go. It was just that Art and Kelly's presence was so much with her when she went.

"Howdy, my friend."

As Theda walked along the empty corridor, science teacher Prince Harney's voice came up behind her. She turned.

"Hello, Mr. Harney."

Female hearts swooned when Prince Harney was around. Harney's students adored him.

Neither Andre, Theda, Angela nor Kitty liked him very much. There was a lot of gossip swirling around the ginger-colored, brown-haired Prince. If his father hadn't been the first principal, if his grandfather were not a millionaire, he might have been fired long ago. But he was still there, married, with two children and a newly pregnant wife. He didn't let his family steal his thunder. He flirted with the students, but didn't really get involved. The female teachers were another matter.

Prince Harney narrowed his pale green eyes. "Please call me *Prince*."

"I prefer Mr. Harney. I might forget otherwise."

He shot her a full, high-voltage look. "U-m-m. You're looking fabulous as usual."

Theda looked at him evenly. "And you're turning heads and breaking hearts as usual. Your compliment box runneth over."

"Don't be so hard on me," he said.

To her relief, the bell rang to change classes and Kitty and Curt came near. She called to them, excusing herself from *Prince* who frowned. He was accustomed to women fawning over him. Theda never gave him the time of day.

Kitty and Curt had wide grins for her and each

other. "I'm going to Mrs. Smith's classroom to ask a couple of questions." She touched his hand. "See you both later."

In her office, Theda and Curt sat down. "I need your help with something," he said immediately.

"Oh?"

"Yes. I want a Hog. That's a Harley-Davidson cycle. Dad's driven one all my life. He thinks I'm too young, but he's crazy about you. If you asked him—I'm sure you could convince him to change his mind."

She sat looking at the youth who was so much like Hunter, but even more like Hunter's father. Charming, handsome, he was already a hands-down winner.

"I hate motorcycles. They're so dangerous," Theda said.

"Not really, if you know what you're doing. I've gone over the stats my dad's always talking about. Accidents are not as frequent as you'd think. Besides, Kitty thinks it'd be cool."

"Kitty's sixteen and so are you," Theda said.

He drew a deep breath, expelled it hard and laughed. "Seventeen in November and don't you and Dad forget it." He hesitated before he said,

"Mom always makes a big thing of my birthdays. She's been campaigning for me to have a Harley since I was fifteen."

The boy's face grew tender as he spoke of his mother and she asked him, "You miss your mother a lot, don't you?"

He nodded. "We're close. Dad and I were both torn up when she left us for another man, but she talked to me, said I'd understand better when I grew up." He rocked himself a little. "Yeah, when I'm a hundred. The dude she married is filthy rich, and their house is a wonder. Piped-in music, no wires showing anywhere. Every electronic thing you can imagine. She wanted me to live with them—I didn't want to, but I really love her a lot."

"That's good. It always makes life easier when we love our parents."

He studied her a moment. "You know, Dr. Coles, it's only been a few weeks, but I've come to think a lot of you. I'm hoping you and my dad can get together the way he tells me you used to be. Said you were his first love. He needs someone. I think he's lonely, but since we came here, he's been a whole lot happier."

They talked about college then and what he

planned to do with his life. He and Kitty would attend Howard. He talked about Harney High and how much he liked it. "Kitty makes all the difference. I've never met a girl like her. Dad says we remind him of you and him."

He paused for a moment and when he spoke again Theda thought he sounded far older. "I don't understand you grown-ups. You can make such a mess of things. He's talked a lot about what you two had since we moved to Crystal Lake. Of course, if you'd married, I wouldn't be here."

She smiled a bit then. "You're going to be all right. I just know it, and I'm sorry about your mother."

He was silent a long while before he said, "Dad told me about my brother who died in the plane crash, told me last night. He cried."

Her head jerked up. She hadn't thought about him telling Curt and she felt her own eyes welling with tears.

"I'm really sorry," the boy said. "You've been through hell."

"Thank you," she said gently, "for being so kind."

Kitty came back then. "You two seem a bit down," she told them.

"Yeah, deep conversation," Curt said.

They were still chatting when Hunter popped his head in Theda's office. The man was eye candy, and Theda felt her pulse quicken.

"Hey, I've been talking with Dr. Coles about my Hog," Curt told his father.

Hunter shook his head. "Won't help. You don't get a Hog until you're old enough to buy one for yourself."

"Ah, Dad, if it's good enough for you…"

"I value your hide more than I do mine."

"It'd be cool riding Kitty around."

Kitty laughed. "Oh, no, you don't. Dr. Coles and my mom have raised me well. I'm not too fond of motorcycles and your dad's right, you should wait."

A few minutes later, after she'd talked with a couple of students, Theda took Hunter into her inner office where they stood just inside the door. He put a hand on each of her shoulders. "I never see you, but I want to kiss you," he told her huskily.

His eyes were tender and hungry. She was honest. "And you know I want you to, but we decided to go slow."

"I love you. I'll always love you." His obsidian

eyes were mesmerizing and the heat from his body blended with hers so that she forgot where she was and found herself in a private fantasy. She almost cried aloud with the intense ache in her whole body for him.

"Okay, I'll keep it slow," he finally said, "but I don't want to. I want to take you in my arms and race somewhere with you, lie with you and make love the way we used to. I used to feel I was so deep into you I was into your very soul and you sure as hell were into mine. Theda…"

"Please don't," she begged him. To change the subject she said, "You told Curt about Kelly."

He nodded. "I meant to talk with you first, but we were talking and it just came up. I don't really remember how. My son loves you the way I do, Theda. Was it all right that I told him?"

"Yes. He needed to know sometime."

"He told me he was glad he had a brother, even if he wasn't alive anymore. He made a copy of Kelly's photo and he's keeping it in his wallet. Like I said, my son loves you. He told me he does."

Theda's body tingled with pleasure. How much the three of them, Hunter, Curt and she, had suffered.

Bracing himself against the passion raging in him, he sat down and she sat beside him.

He drew a deep breath. "I'm taking my cycle out on the back road out from Crystal Lake for a while late this afternoon. Want to come along?"

She eyed him narrowly. "You can bet your bippy I don't. If I had my way, you wouldn't be going, either."

He looked at her thoughtfully. "I'm very careful and I'm very good at riding. I got wonderful pointers from an old Hell's Angels biker. I photographed the group and we became friends."

She turned up her nose a little. "*Hell's Angels.* You always had a knack for making friends with bad guys. In college, you befriended a near thug if I remember."

He roared with laughter then. "Yeah. That guy was from Austin, Texas, and I sympathized with him. But he's no longer a loser. He owns one of the best electronics shops in D.C. I like to think I'm partly responsible for that. We still keep in touch."

"Congratulations," she said drily.

"If you won't go with me, may I stop by on my way back home? If you're busy, I won't stay too long."

"Okay."

"By the way, what are you getting Curt for his birthday?" Theda asked.

"One of several possibilities," he responded, opening his briefcase and extracting several jeweler's boxes. They contained several pairs of cuff links. All of them were beautiful. Theda studied them carefully.

"I like the plain gold ones best, I think."

He bit his bottom lip. "We're in sync. Those are my favorite, too."

She glanced at her watch. She had a meeting at two-thirty with a group of malcontent students, she told him, and didn't look forward to it. They stood and he put the boxes in his case. Hunter's hand splayed against her shoulder and thrills shot through her. *What was she going to do about him?*

"See you later on," he told her.

"Why don't I just cook dinner for you? You've taken me out so much."

His eyes half closed in a mock leer. "Lady, that's an offer I can't refuse."

Chapter 4

"Dr. Coles, I'm calling from Crystal Lake Hospital. Mr. Hunter Davis has been brought in seriously injured. Can you come as soon as possible?"

Sitting in her office, Theda felt her heart lurch. Her stomach felt queasy. "Yes, I'll be there," she managed to say. Her hands were shaking.

Hurriedly snatching up her belongings, she put her cell phone in the pocket of her jacket and rushed out, pausing only to call Angela.

As soon as she hung up with her friend, Curt

Shredded Wheat - 3
Skim Milk - 1 cup - 2
tea - 0
Banana - 2
H2O - 0
brownie 2 (4 mg)

called. "Dad's hurt. The hospital called," he said frantically. "Will you meet me there?"

"I'm on my way."

In the hallway, she bumped into Andre and quickly told him what had happened. "I'm sorry," he said. "Take all the time off you need, but keep me posted." He patted her shoulder. "If there's anything I can do, please let me know."

Theda willed herself to be calm as she drove to the hospital. Once there, she was only half-aware of the people around her. She checked in at the desk, asked about Hunter.

"He was brought in just a little while ago. He's being taken to an exam room. His doctor is Dr. Rita Snyderman. Ask one of the nurses if you need more help," the admitting clerk told her.

She turned to find Curt standing behind her, his wiry body agitated. She put a hand on his shoulder. He was shaking. "We can go up now to the nurses' station and get more information. Please calm down."

"I can't. How badly is he hurt?"

"I don't know, love. I think we'll be able to find out when we get there."

At the nurses' station, a pert blond nurse helped

them. "He was brought in with severe injuries. Severe bleeding. A motorcycle accident."

"Oh, here's Dr. Snyderman," the nurse said. "Let me ask her to talk with you."

Dr. Snyderman was an attractive middle-aged woman. She acknowledged the introduction and shook hands with Theda and Curt, sighing a little. "Well, his injuries are serious, but not as bad as I first feared. There is some internal bleeding. His helmet prevented a brain injury. There are no broken bones, but I'll hold him overnight for observation. One of you may stay with him the night if you choose, although it's not necessary."

Theda could have cried with relief. She thanked the doctor and turned to Curt. "I'll stay, of course. But why don't you stay for a while and then go home and get some rest?"

"I won't be able to rest," he croaked. "Would it be okay if I called to check on him?"

She nodded. "Let me call you."

It was late when a groggy Hunter was brought into the room that held one other man who was asleep. He gave her a wan smile then lapsed immediately into sleep.

Curt hung around until it was late, then left.

Theda settled down into a comfortable chair beside Hunter's bed. Looking at his sleeping form as he snored lightly, she felt love for him fill her body. He was so precious to her. He wouldn't be able to brag anymore that he'd never had an accident on what she thought Curt had rightly called "that damned motorcycle."

She drifted off to sleep after calling Curt to assure him that his father would be fine.

Through the night nurses came to check on Hunter and it was late when the doctor came back. "How's our patient?" she asked.

"Sleeping calmly," Theda told her.

Theda dozed off again a little before dawn, but woke early to find Hunter looking at her, a beatific, if sleepy, smile on his face. "Now I know what I was missing all these years," he said. "Talk about an angel watching over me, angel face."

"You're hopeless. And you're a sick man, so please be quiet," she said. She took his hand and he laced his fingers with hers and pressed hard.

Theda and Curt took Hunter home around noon the next day. Hunter limped a little, but the doctor told them he was doing amazingly well. She requested that he come back for an office visit the following day.

At home once Hunter settled in, with a lunch of New England clam chowder and a garden salad that Theda made for him, she went home and showered, changed clothes and returned to Hunter's house.

She found Hunter and Curt playing Scrabble. Curt was ahead and chortling over it before he grumbled, "I don't know why I let myself get happy. Dad usually wins."

"You're afraid to take risks," Hunter said gently. "You always play it safe."

"Yeah, well, I'm gonna start doing it your way," he said, and laughed. Curt stopped playing as the doorbell pealed and went to answer the door.

Keatha came back with him, stood in the doorway with her hands on her hips. She nodded coolly to Theda and turned to Hunter. "I was worried to death about you. The boy told me what had happened. Maybe you ought to give up that motorcycle, Hunter. Well, I guess you couldn't be too badly hurt if you're home already. How d'you feel?"

"Much better." Almost as soon as she'd come in, Hunter had felt himself getting sleepy. She was a trip, he thought.

"I want you to see that I know when things happen to you. You're a grand substitute for my son, Mort. Now, don't worry about dinner. I'm going to make lamb chops and I'm bringing your whole dinner, with dessert, over and…"

Hunter's eyes opened wide then and he glanced at Theda. "I really thank you, Mrs. Ames," he lied, "but Theda has planned to make country fried white rabbit with all the trimmings and I'm really looking forward to it. She's already marinating the rabbit."

Theda stifled laughter. He seemed so sincere. Keatha's face fell. "Well, I *guess* that's all right." She looked at Theda. "Never thought of you as being much of a cook. My mother always said them as wears tight clothes never can cook."

Theda felt this was a bit much. "I wear form-fitting clothes sometimes, yes," she said, "but I don't think my clothes are ever tight."

Hunter took it up. "Not that I've seen. Nothing wrong with flaunting a superb body."

Keatha changed the subject. "And why don't you call me *Keatha?* These days people aren't making such a big thing about age."

"All right. Keatha it is," Hunter said.

In an effort to get rid of the older woman,

Hunter pled that he wanted to sleep. Mercifully, Keatha took her leave.

"I'll be back. I intend to keep track of you from now on. I won't let you out of my sight," she said. "You're going to be my substitute son." Her voice dripped affection. Hunter forced a smile to his face. He tried to tell himself she meant well, but how fond could he be of someone who so obviously disliked his beloved?

The minute Hunter heard the front door close, he perked up again, grinning broadly at Theda and Curt.

"Hey, I don't think I want to be her substitute grandson. Mrs. Ames can be mean," he said.

"I'll leave you two alone. I'm going to school to hang out with Kitty and the guys," said Curt.

Curt left and Theda sat down by Hunter's bed. He looked her over, his eyes narrowed. "You went home and got even more scrumptious. I really liked the leather jumper, but this wool, formfitting suit is quite fetching," he said, and reached for her.

She swatted him playfully. "Not too tight, I hope."

"Not nearly tight enough. You got that white rabbit marinating?" he asked, and winked.

"You lie so beautifully. Should I look out for that?"

A sober look came onto his face. "I've never lied and I never would lie to you. I was simply trying to carve all the time out for us I can. You can serve me hot dogs for dinner. As long as you're here I don't care."

She bent and kissed his face. "You're sweet," she said. "You always were sweet."

"I believe it if you say it."

They played a couple of rounds of Scrabble and Hunter slept a short while. They listened to a news station on the radio and watched a good mystery on TV.

"I probably should leave early," she said, and Hunter's face fell.

She sat on the edge of his bed and he took her hand. "I want you to stay."

Theda drew a deep breath. "Would that be wise? I can imagine Keatha's tongue wagging about that."

"Who means the most to you, Keatha or me?"

"I think you know the answer to that one, but I've got my professional reputation to protect. I don't want to give Keatha ammunition to shoot me down."

"I'll charm her. Invite her over every night. Call her *Ma*," Hunter said. The boyish smile that curved his lips almost convinced Theda to stay. Almost.

Theda laughed. "I'll stay for a while. They're not expecting the storm to break until around midnight. You'll be fine."

He looked forlorn and her heart went out to him.

After a moment, he leaned over and got a slender tan leather-bound book from the chamber of his night table, handed it to her. She looked at it. Elizabeth Barret Browning's *Sonnets From The Portuguese*. For a moment her heart raced. She had the same book. He had bought a copy for both of them when they were eighteen. They had first read the book in a cove out in Maryland when they were on vacation. And they'd made love afterward. Flames lit her body remembering and she knew from looking at him that he remembered, too.

She found the poem "How Do I Love Thee?" and began reading slowly. He watched her face intently as she read. As he listened, he thought about the time they had lost. Would she fall in love with someone else down the line the way Helena, his first wife, had done? After all, Helena had wanted him so badly in the beginning, and then betrayed him. He shook off all thoughts of Helena and concentrated on the poem and Theda. Her voice was musical, warm.

When she'd finished, he was quiet for a moment. "I want to tell you one thing, ask you another," he said.

"Okay, shoot."

"I want to give you power of attorney in case anything happens to me."

She looked at him sharply. "You want me to…"

"Yes. I trust you more than anyone else. I know you'd take care of Curt."

"Okay, but I'd like you to do the same for me," she said.

"You trust me."

"Yes," she said.

"There's something else," he said. "When I'm fully mobile I want you to go with me up to the Poconos. I've got a cabin up there. It's beautiful. If you could take off on a Friday, we could leave Thursday night and I'd get you back in time for school."

She glanced at him, then lowered her eyes. "Honey, I don't know. We promised to go slow. Alone like that? In a romantic place…"

grinned and took her hand. "There are two
bedrooms. A big one and a smaller one. You can
have the big one. The doors have locks on them
and I'll keep my hands to myself. Promise."

He looked so precious lying there she wanted
to tease him. "I'd go along with little controlled
kisses. You always were a great kisser."

Now, why had she said that? she wondered. He
didn't need reminding.

"Will you go if I promise, and I do."

She drew a deep breath. She needed to get
away for a bit. "When would we go? Oh, yes,
when you're fully mobile. That could take a
while."

"I see the doctor tomorrow. It could be sooner
than you think. Tell me you will."

He was pleading and she never could resist his
pleading. "I'll go." Her voice was little more than
a whisper. "Will Curt be going?"

He shook his head. "I thought he'd jump at the
chance, but he says one of Angela's sons is having
a party and he wants to stay."

"Angela *did* mention it."

She got up and sat on the edge of the bed. "You
always were so persuasive."

She still wanted him as much as she ever had

and it thrilled him to the marrow of his bones. She didn't resist as he pulled her down to him and held her against his chest, feeling the racing beat of her heart and his own heart going crazy. Nothing on earth could have stopped his mouth from going to the hollows of her throat, kissing and licking the soft, tender flesh. There were tears of hot passion in her eyes when his mouth finally found hers and his tongue went deep into the warm, sweet hollows of her mouth. Yesterday was now. Neither thought of the past, only this present that was heaven itself.

Her blood was liquid fire. She couldn't get enough of him. She didn't know she pressed her body hard against his and moaned in the back of her throat. He started to lift her skirt and caress her in her core, but he had made a promise and the devil himself couldn't prevent him from keeping that promise. He had to be true to her and himself, but his whole body ached with wanting to be inside her precious body. He thought of mountain peaks of ice and snow and cold, cold winter waters. Miraculously, it helped.

Gripping her shoulders, he tore his mouth from hers and held her away from him. "We have to wait," he said. "It's the only way."

He held her and studied her face a very long time before she slowly pulled herself together and sat up, sighing. "I guess you really have developed a mature man's control," she said. "We'll know the time is right for us to be together and we can move on once we've gone past the hurt and the torment."

They talked then of Harney, of Curt and Kitty, of Crystal Lake, of Keatha and her shenanigans. And they both knew they talked to slow the flames of passion that raged inside them until they felt they could be together and trust each other not to go too far. Both found it a wonderful feeling, but both ached for fulfillment.

Chapter 5

Hunter healed swiftly with no complications, but it was the third week in October before Theda's schedule would permit her to take a day off again. Now she stood at the back door of his cabin in the Pocono Mountains of Pennsylvania looking out at the valleys below. It was so beautiful this time of year. A light mist hung over the valley. Red- and gold-leafed oaks, yellow spruce, with evergreens still green, it was a vision she'd never tire of watching. She had often vacationed at the resort above them.

Lost in thought, she felt Hunter's big hands squeeze each of her shoulders and she closed her eyes as he kissed the back of her head. After driving all night they'd reached the cabin early in the morning, slept awhile and then washed down hoagies with beer.

She loved the spacious log cabin that Gray Wolf—Hunter's grandfather—had built for him as a replica of his own cabin. It was much cooler in the mountains, so he had made a fire in the big fieldstone fireplace. Now it burned cozily.

"Still tired?" he asked.

"No. It's so beautiful here. I can't wait to see Gray Wolf again."

"And I'm sure he can't wait to see you."

Hunter hugged her and his muscular body pressed in to the back of her. She shivered a little, leaned back against him. "You smell good," she said softly.

"And you smell even better. Like spring flowers and a bit of incense."

"Exactly. You're a sharp one."

"Where you're concerned, I seldom miss."

She wanted to put the few dishes in the dishwasher, but she didn't want to move away from him. "When do we go to Gray Wolf's?"

"Whenever you want. This trip is for you. I want you to have your heart's desire. Your wish is my command. And all the other loving clichés you can think of."

Theda stood thinking of the way she had suffered when her father had died. She thought about the way she still suffered over the loss of her father and mother, her husband and her son. Exactly when did the heart heal from a grievous loss? Hunter had come back to get her and she'd been married, but she couldn't forget the shattered nights she had tossed in agony. Nor the more recent nights when Art and Kelly had haunted her as laughing, loving ghosts. Now Hunter was back in her life and she couldn't truly enjoy him the way she wanted to. Why did she take loss so hard? she wondered. This was not pain, but devastation and she feared it greatly.

People died when they grieved too deeply, or they went mad. Hunter was saying something. She had to ask him to repeat it.

"I asked you what you're thinking."

She withdrew from him then, suddenly afraid of the closeness. Had coming here been a bad idea after all? She was remembering everything the way she had not let herself remember in any real depth before. Just snatches of glory and the pain that followed. The mind didn't take kindly to deep hurt.

She withdrew from his arms and ran the dishes through their cycle while she and Hunter sat on the dark brown bearskin rug in front of the fire.

"The world is full of romantic things," he said, "but few are more romantic than being together near a warm fire in cold weather."

She agreed and leaned back against the brown velveteen foam bolsters he had thrown on the rug along with two big feather pillows. She touched the pillows. "Rose satin. Davis, you really are a romantic."

He grinned. "I got them when we planned this trip. I wanted to surprise you."

Her heart lurched then. Rose satin sheets and pillows were for lovemaking. What did he have in mind? They had said they wouldn't go too far too fast. But she knew that, like her, he lived in memory. In New Orleans where they had gone on spring vacation, there had been rose satin sheets in the wonderful little hotel they'd stayed in. Satin sheets at Hunter's request. She couldn't help smiling.

They spent the rest of the time lazing about,

waiting for the afternoon when they would go to Gray Wolf's for a Cherokee dinner like the one he had served them when they'd visited years before. When it was time to drive over, Theda dressed for warmth in a gray cashmere sweater and matching wool slacks. She fastened gold hoops that Hunter had given her lately in her ears and smiled at herself in the mirror. She looked happy, no doubt about it, but she looked nervous, too.

Hunter was the resplendent male animal in a black, wool turtleneck and black flannel slacks. He whistled long and lustfully when she joined him in the living room. "You're so beautiful," he said.

"I'm not, you know," she said.

"But you are. Theda, you have an inner beauty that you'll never lose. Love and tenderness and sensuality and sexuality go all through you. There's a whole lot of angel in you and just enough hell to make you the most interesting woman I've ever known, angel face. Let's go before we don't want to."

"Ah, you have changed little," Gray Wolf said happily as he greeted Theda and Hunter in his front yard.

He introduced Theda to his wife, Miss Greta.

Dinner was served promptly at four. The meal began with delicious elderberry wine and Theda sipped slowly, savoring it.

"It is the Cherokee dinner of my youth," Gray Wolf said.

Tender wild rabbit with dumplings, green peas with tiny green onions, broccoli, candied yams, macaroni and cheese, garbanzo beans and the ubiquitous garden salad looked very colorful. Gospel music played as they ate.

The meal proceeded at a leisurely pace. When it was over Greta said, "Now, I've got three desserts. We asked Hunter what you preferred and he said peach cobbler. So I made you one, Theda. Double-chocolate-cream cake for Hunter and my husband's choice, blackberry cobbler."

Theda and Hunter thanked her and she went to the kitchen to get the warm cobblers. The cake stood in splendor on the sideboard.

They took their desserts into the living room and ate them there, laughing and talking of the past and their dreams and hopes for the future. Gray Wolf regaled them with stories of his Indian past. He talked about the infamous Trail of Tears when whole tribes of Indians were forcibly

removed from their land and herded into res-
ervations.

"Brave Eagle," he finally said to Theda. "I gave
him that name because I wanted him to go beyond
me." He gazed at Hunter fondly. "And he has. I
gave my great-grandson the Indian name Little
Eagle. And he will be Great Eagle when he is a
man. It is not often we change the names and it is
not our custom, but the boy is different. He is like
you, Hunter, and he will go far."

Gray Wolf gave them three gifts, one each for
Hunter, Theda and Curt. The gifts were all exquisite amulets fashioned of shining silver and polished turquoise.

"These will keep you safe," the old man said
gravely.

Back at their cabin, Theda and Hunter sat on the
front porch and watched the stars and an almost-
full moon. It was very cool and she pulled her coat
more tightly about her. He put his arms around
her and stroked her arm in the coat. As they talked,
lengthening black clouds moved over the sky
and they went in. So much for star watching, he
thought.

Inside, she eyed the fireplace as he relit it and

flames leaped, throwing shadows across the room. He put on a Smokey Robinson CD, then came to where she sat and held out his arms. She rose and went into them. Dancing to the dreamy music, she nestled in his arms and felt thrills sweep through her. So far so good. He held her close, but not too close.

He kissed her face lightly as he had gotten into the habit of doing. "Sleepy?" he asked.

"I am. The mountain air always does this to me. Also, it looks like rain and I always get sleepy when it rains."

They danced a while longer, sipped sangria wine and played a hand of strip poker. He excused himself and left the room to come back in a few minutes holding a navy leather jeweler's case. Sitting beside her, he handed her the case. She opened it. She gasped with delight at the exquisite yellow diamond and platinum ring.

Tears of longing and frustration came to her eyes as he gently placed it on her finger. She shook her head. "You're dreaming, love. You and I are still far away from marriage."

"Okay," he told her, "accept it as a friendship ring. Our birthdays and Christmas are all coming up."

"Thank you so much. For the ring and for understanding."

"You're very welcome." He kissed her then and the kiss caught fire and threatened to consume them, but he exercised exquisite control that left her breathless. She was excited, but finally her eyes refused to stay open and they went to their separate rooms.

She slept soundly until the first flash of lightning lit the room and a crash of thunder brought her wide-awake. She cowered in the dark. Lightning was the one thing that terrified her. Another brilliant strike and another crash and she was out of her bed and running to Hunter. He met her at his door, knowing how afraid she'd be, coming to comfort her. He turned on the light switch but nothing happened. The power had gone out.

He held her trembling soft body against his hard frame and stroked her back as the lightning flashed and the thunder crashed again and again. He pressed her closer.

For a long time the lightning strikes kept coming and the thunder kept crashing around them as the powerful storm awakened in their bodies an intense heat. Her mouth sought his and he kissed her, softly, tenderly at first, then with increasing ardor. His mouth went to the hollows of her throat and he slowly and tantalizingly licked the silken flesh.

Each was remembering the past, reliving it, yes, but living far more in the present. They were in each other's arms and it was *now.* Feverishly, he stroked her back in the soft satin nightgown for a few minutes as heat like none she had ever known flamed through her body. "Please make love to me," she whispered. "It's been so long."

He was silent for a moment before he said, "You're sure this is what you want? We said we'd wait until things are more settled for both of us." His voice was husky, hot with passion, but he was holding back, trying to do what was best for them.

She put her hand on his shaft and pressed it. His gentle touch on her body was driving her crazy. "I don't *want* to think beyond this moment," she whispered. "I want you *now.* I *have* to have you now."

Her mind raced with visions of him inside her.

He got a condom from his trousers, smoothed it on. Then he lifted her and carried her to her bed with lightning still dancing around the room. She felt safe in his arms and her tender body flowered under his touch. Heat so intense she could hardly stand it simmered inside her and his heat led her on. She moaned softly as he positioned her, slid a finger inside, then suckled her breasts hungrily. She tugged at his body, took his shaft in her hand and guided him in.

For a moment, he stopped. "You're going to make me come to the end of this too soon," he said softly. "You don't want that. Slow down."

But she couldn't slow down. Her hips worked in hard concentric circles and her mouth claimed his in a savage kiss she didn't recognize as hers. Greedily, she clutched his hard, tight buns and held him in to her as he exploded.

She took a little longer and he kept working her, stroking her until she shuddered and her body convulsed with the rhythmic contractions of love and wonder. Her tender inner muscles clutched him, then released him again and again, not wanting to let him go.

He stayed inside her a long while. She held him there. The lightning and the thunder had slowed and there was the steady sluice of violent rain against the windows. Finally, he propped himself on his elbow. "I can't think of a time when I've felt better," he said, kissing her cheek.

"Me, too. I'm not going to ask if this was

for the best. Anything this good has to be for the best."

After a long minute, he sighed. "Let me light some candles. There are some in the closet."

"No. Let's just stay like this a little while longer. I'm enjoying the darkness."

And it was much longer before he lit the candles and was rendered nearly speechless at the wondrous expression of love on her face. The cinnamon-colored skin gleamed and her sparkling brown eyes were like the stars they had watched outside.

She salivated as she watched his hard, muscular body and she stroked his pecs and abs. His biceps were developed just right for her taste, not too beefy. Just right. Her fingertips dug into those muscles and he smiled at her.

"I take it you like what you see. If you don't, I'll move heaven and earth to change it."

"I love what I'm looking at. I love you." Her voice was husky, raw with still craving him.

She pushed him back on the bed and he thought tonight she was the aggressive one and it thrilled him. At eighteen, he had taught her all he knew about lovemaking and at thirty-six, she was returning it in spades, with all the ardor of a mature woman.

With him flat on his back, she massaged his scalp, his face and kissed him, going to the thick neck, then to the well-developed chest. Here she licked his flat nipples in concentric circles with a special twist and he shuddered with delight.

He groaned in the back of this throat. "Keep that up," he whispered, "and I'll be your love slave for the rest of my life."

She intensified the licking, then murmured, "Why not?"

Whatever else, he thought, they were partners in passion, always had been. But passion was only part of the game. Pain had slipped in there somewhere and spoiled it. Now pain seemed light-years away and there was only this time and this woman.

He pulled her on top of him, her breasts in his face and suckled them gently, then harder, licking the way she had done. "Hey, I've got more to work with than you had," he teased her. Lord, that had felt good.

His strength came up to her as she lay on him and he entered her and pressed her down hard onto his shaft. He throbbed mightily inside her, his big shaft growing and swelling until it seemed surreal. But she reflected that it wasn't the size of his shaft that made him a winner, but the depth of his love for her.

Surges of pure ecstasy flooded both their bodies. She grew dizzy with the wonder of him inside her, locked her ankles around his and drew him deeper until he was pressed against her womb, a wondrous place and feeling that she wished would never end.

On the plush rug, she got on her knees with him behind her. He kissed the tender flesh of her back and buns and entered the syrupy wet, tight path she made for him. He was all the way in then and a wild cry of savage lust tore from him. Hearing it, she thrilled and her inner walls tightened even more. Tears of pleasure came to her eyes as he kept stroking her back and her buns.

It seemed a long time and yet too soon when she felt the wonder of orgasm and the rhythmic grip and release, grip and release that meant she had to reluctantly let him go.

Thrusting smoothly, evenly, expertly, he thought he knew how the gods of old felt in all their glory as he felt himself flooding her womb with the seed of his passion.

Chapter 6

Early next morning Theda stood again looking out the back door at the wondrous misty scene of the valley below them. She had prepared breakfast and waited for Hunter to come out of the shower. Her body still tingled all over as she thought of the splendor of their night and this morning together. *Had they really made love all night long?*

She heard him come in and was suddenly too bashful to face him. This after waking up in his arms and making love to a coral-and-yellow sunrise like none she had seen before. She felt his arms around her nuzzling the side of her throat as his hot minty breath stirred her.

"We could start all over again," he murmured.

"You're insatiable." She laughed softly.

"And you're not? We're two of a kind. We can't get enough of each other."

"Aren't you hungry?" he asked after a moment of silence.

"Starved."

They ate the scrambled eggs with shrimp, the Canadian bacon, hot buttered grits and wild plum jam with hot buttered biscuits from a prepared mix. They both thought food had never tasted so good.

They had pushed their plates aside and full coffee cups sat before them. She put her foot between his legs, smiling slyly. He caught the foot and massaged it. "You're headed right back to you-know-where if you keep this up," he said.

He smiled at her roguishly. Just then his cell phone rang. It had not rung since they'd been there. It was Curt.

Hunter heard the tension in his son's voice and wondered. "Dad?"

"Yeah, son."

"I started to call you earlier but I didn't want to wake you." Curt went silent.

"I told you to call anytime."

"When're you two starting back?"

"In just a little while. Why? What's going on? Is something wrong?"

"Mom's here," Curt said.

It was Hunter's turn to be tense. "What d'you mean, Curt? Helena's in town?"

"No, Dad, she's *here,* staying with us. She's kind of sick and I told her she could stay at least a little while. I knew you wouldn't want her to, but she's sick and has no place else to go. Please, Dad, let her stay."

Hunter felt his heart fall to his shoes. Damn! And damn again! He needed Helena like he needed the proverbial hole in the head.

"Please don't be mad, Dad. I didn't know what to do. She's divorced, she's alone…and she *is* my mother."

Hunter remained silent.

"Hurry home. I'll, *we'll* be waiting," Curt said.

"We'll be there soon."

Hunter closed his eyes against the shock, then opened them and placed his hand over Theda's. "Bad news," he said.

"I gather from the conversation that Helena's there."

"You gather right. I want you to go by with me before I take you home."

"Don't you want to straighten things out first?"

"There's nothing to straighten out."

She noted the extreme tension on his face and in his body. They hadn't talked much about his life with Helena, but Theda knew that Hunter's wife's betrayal had hurt him badly and threatened his manhood.

He held her hand and stroked it. "She's divorced now," he told her.

She couldn't stop herself from asking, "And how do you feel about that?"

"I don't give a damn what Helena does."

"Hunter, aren't you still in love with Helena, at least a little?"

He shook his head. "When we first married, I was bleeding over you and I felt I came to love her. She claimed to love me more than she ever had anybody and she fed my ego. She got pregnant right away and there was Curt whom we both loved dearly."

He drew a deep breath. "But Helena was very jealous of you. I told her about you early in our marriage and she knew how I felt about you. She said you lived between us. But I made myself love her. She was my wife and the mother of my son."

He squeezed her hand and looked deep into her eyes. "I tried to love her, but in my heart I never stopped loving you."

The trip to Crystal Lake was uneventful and they arrived in record time. It was growing dark when they pulled up; Theda noted that many lights were burning in Hunter's house. She had done most of the driving because she didn't feel he was in any condition to drive. He let himself in with his arm around her shoulders.

Curt and Helena were in the living room and Curt came to Hunter with a whoop, hugging him tightly. "I'm so glad you're here, Dad."

Hunter kept his arm around Theda and nodded coldly to Helena. "How are you?" He didn't call her name. Then his voice warmed. "Let me introduce you to Dr. Theda Coles."

Helena didn't rise from her chair. "How are you, Theda? It's nice to meet you after all these years. Funny, you don't *look* like a home breaker. We expect such women to be glamorous. You're attractive enough, but hardly beautiful…."

"Beauty is in the eye of the beholder," Hunter cut in. "And in my eyes, Theda is a beauty queen."

Helena laughed shortly. "I suppose if you see it that way."

Curt felt caught between a rock and a hard place. He worshipped his mother, but he had become very fond of Theda in the short time he'd known her. "Please don't be mean, Mom," he said. "Dr. Coles has been very nice to me."

Helena felt bile rise in her throat as she looked fondly at her son with narrowed eyes. "You're very easy to love, my son. *We* raised you that way."

Only then did Theda really look at Helena. The woman was movie-star gorgeous with black silk hair that flowed past her shoulders in waves, alabaster skin and fine features. Her eyes were smoky gray and the teeth could have only come from the best orthodontist money could buy. She was glad Helena hadn't offered to shake hands because she would have found Theda's hand cold with dread.

Hunter reached into a canvas bag and withdrew the package Gray Wolf had sent. Curt unwrapped it hurriedly with excitement. He valued his great-grandfather's gifts.

"Hey, this is way cool!" He went to his mother, but her expression was distant and she didn't take the amulet. For a moment Curt looked crestfallen.

"Nice," Helena finally said.

"It's more than nice, Mom. It's beautiful. Kitty's gonna love this."

"And who's Kitty?" Helena asked archly as the doorbell rang.

"A friend," the boy said shortly, and went to get it.

"You can let go of her," Helena said to Hunter after the boy left the room. "She isn't going to run away, the way I did."

By the time Helena had finished her sentence Curt had returned. Hunter's neighbor was standing at Curt's side.

"Well, hello there, you two," Keatha said with saccharine sweetness. "About time you were back. I've helped Curt keep your lovely wife entertained…"

"Ex-wife," Hunter said sharply.

"Oh, yes, I forget. Forgive me. By the way, I brought over some lunch. I guess there's enough for you, too," she said to Theda. She couldn't keep the smirk from her face.

* * *

Curt wished he were away from the whole scene. His heart went out to Theda and he didn't appreciate the meanness with which his mother and Mrs. Ames were handling themselves. Right now, he wanted more than anything to be out of the house and hanging with his friends. He especially wanted to spend time with Kitty.

He didn't remember his mother as being anything like this. But he knew jealousy when he saw it and his mother was jealous. Well, he thought, Theda Coles was a hottie, all right, but his mom was beautiful, too. Even if she wasn't acting beautiful at the moment.

Curt looked over at Theda. She looked as if she felt as he did.

Just then, Theda looked at her watch, said softly to Hunter, "I've really got to get moving."

Hunter smiled at her, his heart in his eyes. "Sure thing."

Neither Theda nor Hunter had removed their coats. Now Theda went to Helena and said, "It's nice to meet you."

Helena made a small sound. "I'll be seeing you around." Her voice was honeyed, smooth and she oozed sophistication. Her eyes on Theda were cold and hostile and said she'd be nothing but trouble.

On the way to Theda's house she asked, "How're you feeling now that you've seen Helena?"

"The way I felt the last time I saw her—angry and bitter. Seeing her made me think about *us*. You and I have always belonged together. Seeing Helena again makes me realize that even more."

At her place, Hunter checked out the house. He went upstairs to her bedroom briefly. He looked at her bed with its quilted rose satin spread and was flooded with visions of them lying on it naked. He hunched his shoulders and shook his head as he came back downstairs. They sat on the sofa and he looked around him, enjoying her beautifully appointed home. "You haven't had a chance to help me get my place together, what with my accident and your schedule."

"Don't worry. I have big dreams for your house."

"My house that is also yours. Everything I have is yours."

"That's sweet. Helena will probably want to stay awhile. Curt said she'd been sick."

His face hardened. "Now, don't you worry. I plan to give her a time limit for my hospitality."

"Curt will want her to stay."

"Yeah, he will, but he's got to face the fact that we're divorced and we're not getting back together."

He bent forward and kissed her brow, then slowly took her in his arms and kissed her passionately. For long moments she gave in to his embrace, then drew away.

"Speaking of limits, you and I are going to have to set some. As much as I want you, I want us to stop making love until we can get things together. Fair enough?"

He looked miserable. "I guess. But you know what they say, everything's fair in love and war." He kissed her fingers. "Okay, we'll stop. I see your point. It's going to be hell now that we've been together. But I'll wait. I want what's best for you..."

"For *us*. And I thank you for being so understanding." She sighed then.

Helena was a beautiful woman, one of the most beautiful she'd seen. She and Hunter had a son between them, a son they both loved. Theda thought, that she, too, had had a son for Hunter. Their dead son was one of the obstacles between them.

As if reading her mind, his eyes went to the large framed color photograph of Art, Kelly and her on the end table. They were at the beach, close to each other, laughing, having fun. He picked it up, held it, studying the faces. "I think about Kelly all the time. Lord, I wish I'd known him, held him in my arms, played with him, watched him grow up." His voice was ragged and she kissed his face.

"I wish he could have known you, too, but let the past bury its dead, I keep telling myself. We're going to have a life together, Hunter. I think we are destined to be together."

"Yeah. I'm certain of that, too. Will you let me kiss you?"

"You know I will. I could never stop you."

He stood up and pulled her to her feet, held her hard against him and kissed her a long time as if he were going away and wouldn't be back for a while.

In bed Theda couldn't sleep in spite of a long, luxurious bath and new silky Egyptian cotton sheets. She kept feeling Hunter's arms around her, his phantom body pressed against her and his sugar-sweet kisses were an aphrodisiac. *What was going to happen to them?* Curt loved his mother and every instinct told her he was going to do everything he could to get Hunter and Helena back together again.

Hunter was afraid of loving again. He admitted it, but he was better at fighting his fear than she was. He would take a chance. But her fear was so strong it mastered her. She knew very well that if she married him and something happened—okay, if he died the way Art and Kelly had died—she couldn't take it. She'd die, too.

She started to call Hunter, but decided against it. She had to fight this out on her own. And she said a fervent prayer that somehow she could work it through.

At home later that night Hunter lay on his back, wide-awake. He and Helena had talked a little when he'd returned. He'd reminded Curt that he had school the next day, and then Hunter had gone to bed. Unable to settle down, Hunter had sat up, punched his pillow and lay back down again. Damn and double damn! He didn't need this grief. He and Theda had a tough enough time working out their fears. But it was typical of Helena to come where and when she was least wanted.

He kept remembering the previous night that had been so different. Cold mountain air, a storm, vivid lightning and thunder, and his beloved coming to him for safety. He had given her a world of pleasure and comfort, as well. He could still feel her tender inner walls gripping his shaft and he closed his eyes and shuddered with rapture. Her soft, lush body was a fevered phantom against him. He swore that he would move heaven and earth to claim her.

Not quite of his own volition, he picked up the phone and dialed her number. When she answered, he mumbled that he was sorry to disturb her, but he'd had to call.

"I wasn't sleep. I *couldn't* sleep, my darling. Couldn't you, either?"

"I keep feeling you in my arms. You're a powerful woman, Theda. *My woman.* Angel face. You've cast a spell on me that won't let go. Do you know that?"

He could hear the smile in her voice. "I know, you've cast the same spell on me. Everything's going to be all right, love. I just feel it in my bones."

They talked until she felt sleep creep into her

system. He said good-night and she hung up the phone.

He fell asleep still smiling and began to dream of the prior night and all the love and passion that still filled them both.

Chapter 7

Theda slept well and woke early. She never needed an alarm. The room was cold because she always slept with the windows open, even in the dead of the wintertime. Now, smiling, she put an arm out from the covers and felt the chilly air. Um-m-m, lovely. She began to get up to close the window when the phone rang. It was Hunter.

"First thing this morning, last thing last night. How's my baby? Did you sleep well?"

His voice was soft and husky, loving. "I couldn't be better," she answered, "and, yes, fire trucks could have blared and I wouldn't have heard them. How are you and how did you sleep?"

"Any better and I couldn't stand it. Look, I'm not going to keep you because I know you've got a busy day ahead of you. Do you have time for lunch?"

"No, but what about dinner?"

"You're on," he said.

"By the way, did you decide how long you will let Helena stay with you?"

"I'll see that she doesn't stay too long. She's had an operation and it didn't go well. She says she didn't heal properly at first and it left her weak. Her doctor finally discharged her. She said she'd find a doctor in D.C. I think she really is sick, honey."

Theda lay thinking that that meant Helena was going to be around for a while and a wave of jealousy swept through her. She quashed it quickly. "Too bad. She looks like the picture of health."

"She's lost weight." Was he defending her? Theda wondered. He had lived with this woman as her husband with a child between them. Such bonds were not easily broken.

She said she had to go, and they decided to eat at her house.

She got out of bed and closed the windows, turned up the thermostat, went to her fitness room and got on her rowing machine. She had all the necessary equipment and used it all, plus calisthenics. She also walked two miles five days a week, rain or shine. She was fit and Saturday night proved it.

Hunter had equipped his exercise room and worked out as ardently as she did. And, boy, was he fit. She giggled at the thought of his powerful lovemaking, then grew sober. If anything happened to them now...

She wasn't going to think about bad things and she set about getting ready for work. Taking a quick shower, she laid out her clothes and went to prepare her breakfast.

Hunter got back under the covers. He planned to sleep a while longer when he heard a knock on his bedroom door. Thinking it was Curt, he said, "Come in."

The door opened slowly and Helena walked into the room wearing a black silk satin robe wrapped tightly around her. "Morning, honey," she began. She was wearing makeup and expensive perfume.

"Get out, Helena!" he roared when he noticed

how she was ogling his bare chest. "I'll put something on," he said.

She advanced as if she hadn't heard him. "Don't be silly. You don't have anything that I haven't seen a zillion times when we lived together."

"Out!" he said again, and she backed away. Hunter had a temper and she had never liked crossing him too much.

"Okay! Okay!" she cried. "You don't have to be so mean about it."

She went out, closing the door and he got out of bed, drew on a pajama top and a flannel robe. She was sure to come back. Helena wasn't to be discouraged when she was after something and every instinct told him she was after him.

She waited a little while and knocked again. This time he went to the door as Curt came down the hall, grinning from ear to ear.

"Hello, Dad, Mom," he said happily, looking from one to the other.

"Curt," Hunter said. His son was way too happy about this situation.

"Hello, baby." Helena went to her son, put her arms around him and kissed him on the cheek.

"Not a baby, Mom. Seventeen next month."

"Oh, I remember. I remember the people I love." She looked enticingly at Hunter who stared at her with cold eyes.

Curt bit his bottom lip. He knew when his father was angry and his father was angry. He began to think of things he could do to make this come out right.

Halfway through what had been an exceptionally busy, but productive day, Theda looked up to see the broad figure of Keatha ahead of her in the school hallway. The older woman huddled with two other women, teachers she knew to have free periods just then. Keatha's voice was harsh and powerful and she didn't keep it down.

"…she's supposed to be guiding youngsters and he's got a teenage son, and she's there every chance she gets."

Theda drew in a sharp breath. Keatha was talking about Hunter and her, she was sure of it. What a lie! She grinned a little inside then. She'd sure *like* to be at Hunter's house all the time, or have him at hers.

She saw the other two women look up and try to signal Keatha that she was coming, but the woman talked on. "Poconos, indeed. You can bet what happened there. Well, his wife is here now."

"I thought he was divorced," one of the women said.

Keatha laughed loudly. "They're supposed to be, but his ex means to have him back and I'm betting on her. She's a beauty. She…"

Theda was even with them then. She nodded and passed on. Both of the women looked thoroughly uncomfortable, though they greeted her pleasantly. She was only a few steps past when Keatha called, "Oh, Dr. Coles. You're going to pass me right by and say nothing?"

"I did speak," Theda said coolly.

Keatha got coy then. She called Theda "Dr." only to rag her, or when she wanted to be especially mean. "Don't you think I deserve a *special* greeting. We see so much of each other nowadays."

"I wasn't aware of that," Theda said evenly.

"Well, hello to you anyway. It's always nice to see you."

Theda lifted her eyebrows and saying nothing else walked on.

In her office, she found Angela waiting for her. She whistled when Theda walked in. "Girlfriend, you are looking on top of the heap. I love that dress and the way you look in it."

"Thanks. You always lift my spirits."

"I just want to check in with you," Angela said. "New development. You know Kitty and I are giving Curt a party in November. As you know, it will be at our house on a Saturday night, so no one has to worry about going to bed early."

"Sounds good to me. You give the best parties I've ever gone to," Theda said.

"And that's a real compliment because you've been to some fancy places." She smiled broadly then, teasing. "Yep, that's quite a compliment."

"You're welcome," Theda said.

"This is really going to be good," Angela said. "Sparkling cider punch with huge imported-from-South America strawberries!"

"Sounds good."

Theda told Angela about what had just happened with Keatha. Angela grimaced. "God will forgive me, but I hate that woman. If she's His handiwork, it doesn't show."

Chapter 8

Hunter was having dinner with Theda the following Sunday night and he came loaded down with cameras. She greeted him at the door with a kiss. He had his own key and she had a key to his house.

He was very excited. Setting the equipment down, he grinned. "Have you got a backless bra?"

"No, I'm not that daring. Why?"

"Honey, I hardly slept last night, but I wanted to be looking at you when I told you my dream. I just got commissioned to do a one-man show at a prestigious gallery next spring. The show will be all pictures of you. You're my greatest inspiration. And guess what? Another photo gallery in New York's Village is also interested in featuring my one-man show."

Theda laughed and hugged him again. "Whoa! How can you be sure the photos will come out the way you want them to?"

"These are in my bones. They can't, they won't fail." He held her at arm's length for a few minutes, then kissed her brow. She was so hungry for him to hold her, and thrills raced through her body as he pulled her close. "Maybe I don't need dinner. Food isn't what I want just now. You look so good. That color is you."

Watermelon silk and wool jersey was what she wore, draped and outlining her broad hips and narrow waist and her high, full breasts.

"We said…" she began and he finished for her.

"…we'd wait and we will. There's no law against wanting and, baby, I want you in the worst, or the best way. Okay, you're in luck. When I work, that's where my mind is. And as soon as we get through dinner, we can begin. Do you have a cream or vanilla-colored or off-white dress, preferably a ball gown? I should have checked all this out before coming."

"You know, I don't. I do have a couple of ball gowns, but they're all in dark colors. I do have a length of ivory silk velvet that I picked up in New York to make a gown for the Harney Christmas Ball. Would that do?"

"It sure will. I want to do your beautiful back, just the back from many angles. Like Duchamp's *Nude Descending a Staircase.*"

"I like the idea." She was getting as excited as he was. She went to her bedroom, dug the fabric out from her dresser and took it back to him.

He unfolded the lush velvet and took a deep breath. "Perfect for now. But I want you to get a backless bra. You'll have to go through a lot of sittings. And we really need an ivory gown."

"Look, I can borrow one from the dressmaker in town. How long will you need it?"

"A week at the most. Borrow the most beautiful one you can find, off the shoulder with long, fitted sleeves."

"Will do, and I'm hungry even if you're not."

"I'm hungry for you *and* the meatballs. They smell really good." He sniffed the air and winked at her.

She had set the table in the dining room to make the dinner special. She lit the room with candles and she placed a pink gladioli and fern centerpiece on the table. Dinner was simple: whole grain spaghetti and ground sirloin meatballs. The sauce was her specialty with thick chunks of tomatoes, onions and green peppers. The wine was his favorite chardonnay.

Looking at her, he loved the way the candlelight highlighted her hair and brought out the tinted red, brown and gold of her cinnamon-colored skin. She picked up a hot buttered slice of soft French bread and smiled at him. "What're you thinking?"

"X-rated thoughts about you."

"Oh, really."

They ate slowly, savoring the meat dish and the tasty vegetable salad they both favored. Dessert was small slices of cherry cheesecake.

"I saw Curt today. He looks stressed," Theda said after they'd finished eating.

"With reason. Helena is really putting the heat to him. He tells me she wants to get back together with me," Hunter said.

"And what do *you* want?"

He answered without hesitation. "You know what I want, love. You, and you alone."

She hesitated. "Hunter, what are you going to do about Helena?"

Only then did he tell her about Helena coming into his room.

"She really does want you back then."

"It was already too late when she left," he said sadly.

He reached over and took her hand, squeezed it hard. "Beautiful ring, lady. A man who loves you very much gave it to you, I'll bet."

"He says he does. I know I love him with all my heart."

As Hunter worked with Theda, he explained what he wanted to do. "This will take a series of settings. I'll get the bare outlines done tonight, but I need studio lighting to create the angles and forms I want in your photos. You'll need to come to my home studio and sit for me there."

"I've been skittish about coming by with Helena there."

"I know, and I'm doing something about that. In the meantime, use your key any time you want to come over."

"You're aware there's gossip about you and me."

"No, but I'm not surprised. Perhaps we should get engaged. Would you like that?"

She shook her head. "Not yet. I'm still too mixed up. And that might hurt your son. Curt needs a chance to work this through with his mother. He loves her."

"Adores her. Always has. But he's fond of you, too."

"I'm beginning to love him no matter what happens."

"Nothing's going to happen except we're going to be together."

He picked up the photo of Art, Kelly and her. "You took this?"

"Yes."

"You have an eye for photography, a natural bent. Now, let's go to work."

He posed her in a long-sleeved navy satin dress and unzipped it to the waist. He used a Polaroid camera and digital cameras to take pictures he would print out on his computer. When the instant photos came out, she gasped. They were gorgeous. She didn't see how the lighting could be any better, but he assured her that she would be astounded at the difference.

Her back was still bare at the end of two hours of exhaustive shooting and he put his camera aside and came to her. Bending, he kissed her back, running his tongue lightly up and down as she shuddered with vivid pleasure.

"Did you know the tongue packs the heaviest punch in the human body?" she asked him.

"No. Where'd you learn that?"

"From my dentist."

"I'll guard my tongue. I don't want to hurt you ever."

"It only hurts me when I'm without you."

He pulled her up then and his tongue went deep into the honeyed hollows of her mouth as he held her trembling body hard against him. Then he told her, "You'll never be without me again."

She fought the fear that kept her from fully belonging to this man, and she knew he had demons of his own. And now there were Curt and Helena to consider.

"What's going to become of us?" she asked him.

"We're going to be fine."

At Hunter's house, Helena smoothed the top of Curt's head as she stood behind him at the kitchen table where he drank a cup of chocolate.

"Hunter's late. Have you done all your homework?"

"Sure have, that and more. I'm way ahead."

"Are you seeing Kitty tonight?"

"Next weekend. We're going to a movie. She wants to see that new 'chick' flick."

Helena raised her eyebrows. "That's a pretty sophisticated movie for kids your ages."

"Yeah, I guess, but Kitty's a sophisticated girl in spite of the fact that her mother keeps her close," he said.

"You're serious about Kitty, aren't you?"

"I sure am."

"Curt?"

"Yeah, Mom."

She hesitated a long moment. "I messed up big-time with your father. Now I know how much I love him and I'd like us to get together again. You'd like that, wouldn't you?"

She had walked around and sat opposite him. "You bet I would." His heart leaped at the thought. The family together again. He thought of Dr. Coles then. She would be hurt, but she'd get over it. He told himself she'd be fine, and his mother deserved forgiveness. He'd forgiven her so why couldn't his father forgive her? he wondered.

"You've grown up into a wonderful boy. Do you know how much I love you and your father?"

"I think I do. And we… Well, I love you. Dad's in a spin about Dr. Coles, but he'll get over it."

She looked at him imploringly. "Will you help me get him back?"

"What can I do?"

"Talk to him. Tell him you want us to go back together again. We used to have so much fun together. Remember?"

"Yeah. I remember. Mom, you know something?" He drank the last of his chocolate.

"Yes, love?"

"You're really beautiful. You've got to come to the school sometime so I can show you off."

She looked at him with pleased surprise. "You'd like that?"

"I'd love it. Mrs. Ames is at the school all the time. She could introduce you around."

Helena sat musing with her eyes narrowed. Keatha would love that and she had plans for her budding friendship with Keatha. She'd stay here a while longer, then rent a house in the neighborhood close to this one. Keatha had told her there were a couple that would be for rent. Keatha was going to be her lifeline.

"I'll do it. You know, you're free to use my car whenever you wish."

He looked up, eyes shining. "You mean it? That's a bad car you're driving."

Helena drove a lipstick-red sportscar and she couldn't decide whether she or the car looked sportier. She sat with her robe around her and the garment fell away, exposing her lacy black slip and her shapely legs. Hunter thought she was too careless in her dress around Curt, but she liked making men's eyes light up, even her son's. She leaned back and half closed her eyes. Who was Hunter fooling? He had been turned on when she'd gone into his room. She knew all the signs.

Curt went to bed and Helena stayed up until after midnight when she heard Hunter's car coming into the garage, then she got up. She lightly licked her lips, a smile played about her mouth and her eyes were lit up.

Going up the stairs she listened for the front door to open and when it did, she raced down the hall, pulled off her robe and flung it in her room. Then in the beautiful black lacy slip she gave a mock gasp as Hunter came into view. He carried his photography paraphernalia.

"Oh, I wasn't expecting anyone," she said softly.

He looked at her coldly. "Obviously. Is Curt in bed?"

"Some time ago."

"Good. I hope you weren't walking around like that around him."

She came up the hall and moved closer to him. "You're such a fussbudget. Relax. Let me help you with that gear. Our son is a big boy now.

"My point exactly. Go to bed, Helena. It's late."

"Did you have fun? And do let me help you. I used to."

She was getting under his skin and she stood in his path. "The past isn't prologue in this case," he told her coldly.

"Don't be mean. I can't help loving you, Hunter. We had it all once."

Hunter didn't want to hear it. He pushed her aside and went down the hall into his studio and closed the door, locked it.

There had been a time when they'd have been in each other's arms, but he didn't want her anymore. Or did he? He felt sorry for her. She had lost a man she loved because Hunter had hurt her body grievously. She hadn't accused him this time in so many words, but it was there between them. He had ruined her life and she said she'd forgiven him, but could he forgive himself?

He pulled the rough and the finished Polaroid

copies from his backpack and looked at them one by one. How could a simple human back be so gorgeous? He felt a thrill go through him as he closed his eyes and in fantasy felt Theda's flesh under his arduous stroking. Thinking about her brought on an erection that was painful and he pressed it down. One week ago they had made intense, raging love in a storm in the mountains. She had cried with joy and he had felt like crying. He didn't think again of Helena. She was part of his past, as Theda was even more a part of his past. But Theda was also his present and his future.

When he opened the door an hour later, Helena sat huddled on the floor across from his studio in her robe. She got up as he opened the door. "I have to talk with you," she told him.

"Helena, it's late. I'm sure this can wait."

She shook her head, going close to him again. He could smell the oriental musk perfume she wore. "It can't wait, my darling. Please, Hunter, give us a chance. Make love to me again. I need you. It's been so long since a man held me. I said I forgive you, but when men know about me, they don't desire me anymore. You didn't intend to hurt me, but you did and I know you're sorry. It's such a small thing. Theda need never know. I'm going crazy wanting you…."

"Stop this nonsense, Helena. You know this can never be." But he was seeing her face again at her sister's house when she'd asked him to come there and she'd told him. They'd been separated then and already she had a new love, richer, more powerful. And she'd lost that new love after marrying him when he'd found out what Hunter had done to her. Would he never be free of this?

But he knew there was nothing on earth he could do about it now. If he were to take her, it would hurt Theda too much and he was never going to do that. And right now he didn't want her. He wanted Theda and Theda alone.

She was crying then. Helena had always cried to get what she wanted and it had worked on many men, beginning with her father. Yeah, he thought, he felt guilty to the bone, but this was a dangerous situation and he didn't intend to let it go further. His mind was made up as she moved even closer and he backed away.

"Helena, I can't let you stay here any longer."

"But I have no money to go somewhere else." She sounded desperate. "You know Jack's tied my money up in court and I'm almost destitute. Where would I go?"

"No problem. I'll rent an apartment for you, pay for it. I owe you that."

"I have many expensive things coming here out of storage when I get settled. I need a house."

"Okay. There are houses available in Crystal Lake. I'm going to get on this immediately because you've got to be out tomorrow!"

But Helena was not to be stopped. She came closer with her lips parted. "Please kiss me. I'll make you know that we can be together again. You still love me. I know you do. And I love you."

"Go to bed, Helena!" he thundered.

He was glad Curt's bedroom was at the other end of the hall because he knew his son wanted them together again. He felt sorry for his son, but this was one game he wasn't going to win. With a hurt look, Helena went into her room.

In bed Hunter tossed. He wanted to call Theda but he couldn't call her for every little thing that went wrong. Helena was pulling out all the stops. She knew very well how guilty he felt, but this time the guilt card wasn't going to work. He had Theda to consider now. It was two o'clock in the morning before he fell asleep to dream of Helena wrapped around him, a hellish hag hanging on to him relentlessly. Then she changed into the beautiful woman Helena was and she was his wife again and he was crying bitter tears because she was telling him she was leaving him for another man and his heart was breaking.

The sun was bright when he came awake to Curt banging on his door and breathlessly coming in. "Dad, please come help me with Mom! She was getting me breakfast and she passed out. I got her to the living-room sofa, but she's in a bad way."

Chapter 9

A pale Helena lay moaning on the sofa. Hunter knelt and felt her pulse, put the back of his hand on her forehead. She seemed to him to have a little fever. He sat back on his haunches.

"What was she doing when she fell?" he asked.

"She had put a cup of coffee on the table and started to sit down. She said her head was hurting. Dad, what's wrong with her?"

"I can't tell, son." He glanced at his watch. Most doctors didn't make house calls.

Helena breathed deeply and roused. "What happened?" she murmured.

"You fainted. Has this happened lately?"

She nodded. "A couple of times." She tried to sit up.

"No, don't," Hunter said. "We'll wait a few minutes and if you don't feel better, I'm taking you in to the hospital."

"No. I'll be all right. My head hurt all night long. Remember, I've got to move today."

"That can wait."

Her voice sounded weak, plaintive. "You're sure. I want to do the right thing. You've got your work to do. I don't want to be in your way."

"You're not in the way, Mom." Curt's face was shadowed with anxiety. She had told him Hunter wanted her to leave.

In a few minutes Helena insisted on sitting up. "This is old stuff to me. I'll survive, believe me." She gazed at Hunter with adoring eyes and whispered, "Thank you."

Hunter felt uncomfortable. Helena was a master manipulator and he wondered if she were really sick or if this was just another ploy. Hunter got a thermometer and took her temperature. It was normal.

"Honey, please get me a glass of water?" she told Curt.

After he left, she turned to Hunter and touched his face. "You were always so good with me when I had these headaches. One doctor in New Mexico thinks I might have a brain tumor, maybe cancer. I just never went back. I've missed you, Hunter. Lord, how I've missed you."

Hunter shook his head. "Don't talk. Save your strength. Helena, I'm going to talk to a doctor and get a referral. I want you to have a comprehensive physical exam. You've been through a lot."

Helena had told him about her father's death and his money being tied up in the courts through bankruptcy the way hers was from her divorce. Talking about it had brought back Hunter's father's bankruptcy and death.

"With you on my side, maybe it was all worth it." She smiled wanly.

Curt came back with a slice of buttered toast and some almonds. "You didn't get a chance to eat anything."

"I'm not hungry, but I probably need something." She nibbled on the food and Hunter patted her shoulder and went out. Curt continued to hover over her.

Hunter called the doctor who had treated him after his accident. To his surprise she answered. She was already in her office and it was only eight o'clock. Her cheery voice was welcome. "How's one of my favorite patients?" she asked him.

He quickly told her what had happened and she mulled it over. "I have a colleague, a Dr. Lucy Fields, that I'd like to see her. She's an early bird like I am, so call her right away and I'm sure she can see your ex-wife today, at least for a brief visit."

Dr. Fields was also in and he made arrangements for her to see Helena that morning.

He called Theda then and told her what had happened. He also told her that Helena could be faking. It had happened before. "But she's always had monster cluster headaches and a few migraines." He told her about the possibility of a brain tumor or worse, cancer.

Theda felt her heart plummet. She didn't know what to think and she wondered at the deep concern in Hunter's voice.

"Is there anything I can do?" she said, noting that he hadn't asked.

"I don't want to interfere with your work."

"I can and will make time. You know that."

"I've just got to make sure she's all right. I told you last night I was asking her to leave and I did. I'll do everything I can to help her, but she can't stay here, love. It just won't work."

Theda felt some semblance of relief then. "I'll help in any way I can. How're you feeling?"

"I *was* feeling on top of the world. I always feel that way when I've got a prime subject and photos to be shot. Honey, I want to strike with these sittings with you while the iron in my mind is hot, but I think we should wait until this business with Helena is resolved. It's killing me to wait, but you understand."

"I understand and like I said, if there's anything I can do…"

"I love you so much."

"And I adore you. Good luck with Helena and keep me posted."

"You know I will. Okay if I come by very late this afternoon?"

"Oh, yes. But I understand if you need to stay with Helena."

"I need to see you. Curt will be home and I'm sure Keatha will be over to look after Helena. I'll only be fine if I can hold you."

His words took away some of the anxiety she

felt. Helena was a beautiful woman and she packed a sensuous wallop. He had married this woman, had a child with her who wanted them together again. She was the outsider and it hurt.

At the hospital in Dr. Fields's office, Hunter and Helena sat side by side facing the doctor who glanced at the papers before her, then looked up with a bright smile. "Mr and Mrs. Davis. Suppose you tell me your symptoms, Mrs. Davis."

Hunter knew a moment of anger. Helena had put down his last name with her first name. Damn it, she was playing games again. He shook his head vehemently. "She's my *ex*-wife. Her last name is Ware. She'll tell you her symptoms."

Helena shot Hunter a smug look. "Just dealing in fantasies, honey," she said as the doctor looked from one to the other.

Helena refused the comprehensive, saying she had had one little less than a year ago. She would submit to a general exam. The doctor reluctantly went along with that, but insisted that she have another CAT scan just in case there was something adverse continuing to happen with her brain. Helena could have the simpler tests that morning and a couple that afternoon, then return for the CAT scan the next day.

"So that's it," the doctor said. "Let's begin."

To Hunter's surprise and dismay, Helena looked at him with frightened eyes that didn't seem to be fake at all. "You'll stay with me, won't you? Hunter, I'm so scared."

He nodded. "Yes, I'll stay."

"Thank you."

He wandered the corridors of the hospital as Helena underwent the tests. He called Theda, who was having lunch. "How's it going?" she asked.

"Helena's scared and I've never known her to be frightened about her health." He had been going to say he had never known her to be frightened before, but he remembered all too well when she *had* been badly frightened on a lonely North Carolina road—frightened of him. But he wasn't going to think of that now.

He went out to his car and made a series of business calls.

Yeah, he was edgy. Visions didn't come every day and he wanted to give this one his best shot. Funny, Theda had come to him in a dream, sitting for him and in the dream he had unzipped her dress and exposed her beautiful silken brown back with the brown mole on one shoulder and he had known that it was a prize shot, like no other he had done.

He talked with Theda again later. "Assure me that I'm not driving you crazy," he told her. "I'm really nervous about this. Baby, I don't know what I'll do if something is really wrong with her. Will you stand by me?"

She didn't hesitate. "You know I will." But she groaned inside. He really *was* concerned and she could imagine what Curt was going through.

"Thank you. We were made to be together."

Reluctantly, Hunter hung up. Curt walked into Theda's office seconds later. His face looked drawn and anxious. "Could I talk with you a minute?" he asked.

When she nodded and asked him to have a seat, he was silent a few moments. "Mom's sick," he told her. "Dad's asked her to leave." Plainly, he put the two things together. "God, I hope there's nothing really bad wrong. I'm just getting her back again." He looked up then, flustered. "Look, I know how you and my dad feel about each other, but she's still in love with him and I think a part of him is still in love with her...."

He looked up then, tears in his eyes. "Could you give them a chance?"

She met his gaze squarely. "But, my dear, that's up to Hunter."

"No. No, it isn't. If you backed off, gave them a chance…"

His voice drifted then and she felt sorry for him, but she felt sorrier for Hunter and for herself. Was Curt right? *Did* a part of Hunter still love his ex-wife?

She was going to be honest. "I can promise nothing," she said evenly. "I love Hunter and I believe he loves me. Ours is an old love and we deserve each other." Then she drew courage from the facts of the case. "Your mother left him for another man. He's still hurting over that. He had given her no cause to leave…."

"He was always traveling," Curt blurted out. "She said she was lonely."

"He wasn't traveling when she decided to leave. She fell in love with another man and she left him—and you."

"I can forgive her and I think he can, too."

She shook her head. "I don't see it that way. It isn't a question of forgiveness."

"Look, I like you a lot. I was coming to love

you, but I love my Mom more. I wanted you and Dad to marry, but things have changed now. Please think it over. You don't want a man who loves another woman."

Theda laughed a little then on the edge of mild hysteria. Oh, yes, she *did* want Hunter, even if he still loved Helena. If Helena was going to fight for him, then she was going to fight, too. Because she knew that Helena was a manipulative, treacherous woman who could not help hurting Hunter again if the opportunity ever presented itself.

On the way to Theda's late that afternoon, Hunter wanted time to sort out his thoughts. Traffic was bad, giving him the opportunity he needed. He was tied up in knots with his visions of the photos he wanted to take pressing in on him. Thoughts of Theda filling his mind with luscious pictures were crowded by unwanted thoughts of Helena. He could hardly wait to get to Theda's comforting warmth. When he finally reached her house, he didn't use his key but rang the bell.

When she opened the door, her face was solemn. "What's wrong with your key?"

"I didn't want to interrupt anything by barging in on you. You look beautiful."

He took her in his arms and held her for long moments, then nuzzled her throat and kissed her hard and thoroughly. "You're enticing me, you know."

"Um-m-m. Is that a bad thing?"

"What do *you* think?"

She leaned back in his arms and looked at his dear face, then stroked his smooth skin. "Don't they say that all's fair in love and war?"

Her heart was beating overtime. She was shaken when she finally drew away from him. "How is Helena? What did the tests show?"

He drew a deep breath. "So far so good. All the tests have been normal, but when Helena described recent symptoms, the doctor thought there might be a brain tumor. She has a CAT scan scheduled for tomorrow."

His voice sounded warm and tender and she felt her heart slow with anxiety. "You sound so worried."

"Yeah, I am. I told her she'd have to move. Now this comes up. But she's acting damned decent about it. At first I thought she was pulling a stunt to keep from moving, but maybe not."

Theda still thought Helena might be pulling a stunt. "You said you'd find her a place."

He laughed shortly. "It looks like that won't be necessary. Keatha insisted that she stay with her as long as she wants and Helena is delighted."

"How do *you* feel about that?"

"I'm not happy about it. But, of course, Curt is on cloud nine. Keatha's always made her house available to us, but the woman makes me uncomfortable."

His face was grim as he talked. He wasn't a happy camper. "Is that chili I'm smelling?"

She laughed. "Hot as hell and twenty times more delicious. The way you like it. I hope you'll have dinner with me."

"I was just here last night," he said.

"I never get tired of you."

"Same here," he said.

"Don't touch me again or we'll never eat dinner," she warned him.

"I'd say that's a good trade-off."

While eating dinner, Theda told him about Curt's visit and he looked at her sharply. "He's unhappy. That's for certain. But then he's had unhappiness in his life before. I had to remind him that he was unhappy when she left us. He doesn't want to talk about that. But don't worry, Curt likes you a lot," Hunter assured her.

KIMANI PRESS™

An Important Message from the Publisher

Dear Reader,

Because you've chosen to read one of our fine novels, I'd like to say "thank you"! And, as a special way to say thank you, I'm offering to send you two Kimani Romance™ novels and two surprise gifts – absolutely FREE! These books will keep it real with true-to-life African-American characters that turn up the heat and sizzle with passion.

Please enjoy the free books and gifts with our compliments...

Linda Gill

Publisher, Kimani Press

off Seal and Place Inside...

PUBLISHER'S
FREE GIFTS
SEAL
THANK YOU

Two NEW Kimani Romance™ Novels
Two exciting surprise gifts

PLACE
FREE GIFTS
SEAL
HERE

168 XDL ELWZ

368 XDL ELXZ

FIRST NAME

LAST NAME

ADDRESS

APT.#

CITY

STATE/PROV.

ZIP/POSTAL CODE

Thank You!

"Or *did*. Right now, he can't see anything but Helena," she said.

"That's too bad. He's old enough to know that I have a right to be happy." He picked up her hand and kissed it. "And you make me happy."

He seemed bothered now, as if there were something he couldn't quite thrash out and wanted to. "I'm not going to pose you in my studio. Caitlin Steele, the woman who is sponsoring my one-man show, has offered me a studio at her gallery. Excellent lighting, maybe better than I've been able to get mine to be. You can store the gown there and stop by after school. We'll do it after hours and you'll get a chance to meet Caitlin."

"I've heard of her. They're in the Adams Morgan area. Her gallery and her home."

"Yeah. She and Marty have twins. Something I'd like to have with you."

Her womb expanded when he said it and pure honey filled her veins. "Are we ever going to get past our fears of being hurt too badly to stand it? I know mine haven't gone anywhere."

He looked grave. "I'm a risk taker, love. I admit, I can't love you again yet the way I want to, the way we both deserve, but I'd take a chance…"

She shook her head. "I can't do that. The memories are still too strong. I was afraid of dying from the hurt. Can you understand that?"

He nodded. "After having been there and done that, I can." He thought for a while about what he had said and changed the subject. "The chili was just what I needed—and you."

A delicious thrill went the length of her body. "When you say it that way, I'm sorry we decided against making love."

"*You* decided."

"Oh, you!" She balled up her fist and cuffed him lightly. "We both did."

"I lied. My body doesn't like that decision at all." Then he changed the subject again. "Getting back to Helena, I keep dreading bad news."

She frowned, wondering if he knew how deeply concerned he looked when his ex-wife's name came up. There was everything warm and caring now when he spoke about her. Theda was getting very worried....

Chapter 10

At Harney High the next morning in her office, Theda sat talking with Angela. They were discussing Helena's illness. "Talk about your bad timing," Angela said, "Curt's birthday party is only a little over a week away."

"I've been thinking about that," Theda said slowly. "I'm waiting to talk with Kitty. And, of course, we'll know today something about just what's going on with Helena, or at least Hunter hopes to know."

"Honey, I hate to even bring it up, but gossip

is breaking out all over. We're enough of a small town, even if we are a small city, to people watch. And you and Hunter are glamorous people."

Theda shrugged.

"Ladies." Kitty came into the room, her attractive young face somber. She drew a deep breath and took the seat Theda offered. "You know about Curt's mom. Well, I've been thinking and we've been talking about his birthday party. He doesn't want to have it if she's in any kind of trouble."

Theda nodded. "I expected him to feel that way. We can always have the party some other time."

"Yes," Kitty said. "He's really taking it hard. He's crazy about his mom." She looked at Theda and held her breath a moment.

Her face was suddenly shadowed with anxiety. "I hope Curt's mom is all right."

"So do I," Theda said.

After Angela and Kitty left, Theda began to work on a batch of student background folders for at-risk kids when Andre came in.

"What's on your mind, Andre? And please do sit down," she said.

He sat down and was silent a long while before he spoke. "I need to have lunch with you today. We still have business to take care of, and we need to discuss some aspects of your taking over as principal next year. I may be leaving this summer and you'll have summer school, as well."

"Of course."

He seemed a bit uncomfortable. "Theda, I've begun to hear a bit of gossip about you. We have to remember that Crystal Lake is a small city, with the emphasis on *small*."

She looked up sharply. "I've been careful, I've thought. No overnight sojourns. No PDA. After all we have to be considerate of Hunter's son's feelings, too."

"I know you've tried to be discreet," he said. He expelled a harsh breath. "His ex-wife's presence in his house is complicating things, isn't it? I've met her and I'm impressed. Isn't she a problem for you?"

"Somewhat. She won't be living with him much longer."

"I'm glad to hear that. I've talked with Keatha Ames a lot lately trying to smooth things over. It seems she's become very, very fond of the woman."

Theda raised her eyebrows. "You're probably better off saving your breath."

Again that morning Hunter paced the halls of Crystal Lake Hospital. Helena's doctor touched his arm. "I know how worried you are and the doctor whose handling the CAT scan has promised to take time to do a preliminary check with the lab this afternoon and if nothing looks suspicious, he can and will say so. You wanted to be kept advised of the particulars, so check in with my office and I'll talk with you."

Helena came to him in a scarlet jacket and black miniskirt. She smiled sweetly, took his hand and pressed it. "I'd almost forgotten what a treasure you are."

He didn't reply.

She glanced at her watch. "There's been a bit of a delay. I go in at eleven now instead of ten. I can't help thinking, Hunter. What if I *do* have a brain tumor or cancer? I have no one but you and Curt. Would you stand by me then? Just until it's over, one way or the other. Remember when I used to get hysterical when I was angry at you and threaten suicide?"

He looked down at her hand on his arm. "Helena, don't borrow trouble. Let's cross that bridge when we get to it."

"Please walk me to the door. My knees are shaking so badly I can hardly walk."

In a kind gesture, he put his hand under her elbow and she gazed up at him with an ingratiating smile. "Thank you for everything." And he couldn't be sure, but he thought she added, "my darling."

Back in the hallway, he sat on a marble bench and for the first time in a couple of hours had a chance to think of Theda. Theda was in his blood like a raging fever. Only there was no cure for this fever.

His face hardened as he thought about Helena. She was plainly terrified and he wondered what he *would* do if she were as sick as she was afraid she might be. Theda would always stand by him. Curt would be devastated. And Helena was the kind of woman who could hurt herself rather than live with brain tumors or cancer. He didn't want to think about it, but he had to think about it.

By two that afternoon, Theda felt she'd lived through a couple of days. Her mind was on Hunter and what was to come. She knew she'd stand by him if Helena was seriously ill, but what was in store for him and her?

She had a few minutes alone when the phone rang. Hunter. "It's all over, sweetheart. The doctor is ninety-nine percent certain there's nothing wrong. Are you too busy for me to come by?"

"No, please do." She was going to have to shift around a couple of appointments, but she meant to see him.

He sounded so excited. "I have to take Helena home, get her settled. I don't have to tell you she's none too pleased about this. I should be there in a couple of hours. Just wait for me. The school day will be over. I want to go somewhere with you."

After she hung up, Theda felt the heavy weight of anxiety lift from her shoulders and she could breathe freely again.

Hunter came with a florist's box and a big grin. He kissed the corner of her mouth. "I must have done something right. This is all I could hope for. Formal test results come back tomorrow, but the doctor says the brain surgeon studied the X-rays and assured her there was nothing to worry about. This seems to simply be a case of nerves."

"I'm so relieved."

"So am I. Open your roses."

"I'm going to take them home."

He shook his head. "No, I want you to enjoy these here. There's a box of gorgeous peonies in the car for your house."

She got water from the bathroom and quickly arranged the roses, brought them back and set them on her desk. He was at the windows. "It's a beautiful day after all," he said softly.

He explained then that they would take her car and his to Caitlin Steele's gallery in D.C. She knew where it was.

It was almost closing time when they reached The Costner Art Gallery and the delightful woman Hunter introduced her to. Caitlin Steele and her husband, Marty, were superb artists and ran one of the best galleries on the East Coast.

"He keeps talking about you," Caitlin told her. "Meeting you, I can see why. I have the studio all set up for you. It's on the second floor. Marvelous skylight and the lighting is superb by any standard. Feel free to use it for as long as you like. The last artist to use it was blown away by it."

Caitlin showed them around the gallery. "Several groups of school kids are touring the gallery. We're getting more and more of them and I'm, oh, so pleased. The growth of this country lies in its kids and we want them to have the best possible education in the arts." Both Caitlin's and Marty's paintings hung here. A large alcove held an exhibit of the Black Eagles, Tuskegee's famed black airmen from WWII. They exclaimed over this superb showing of photographs that depicted a time long gone that had held such promise and glory and such heartbreak.

"I know you've got great plans for these photos," Caitlin said. She laughed as she commented to Theda, "His face lights up when he talks about his dreams, and I've seen what happens when Hunter has dreams. I'm really into his show with me in the spring. And Hunter's book sells briskly here. You both look really happy. There's nothing like pleasant anticipation."

"Believe me, I am happy," Hunter said. "I've just about got the world on a string."

"And I'm happy." Theda felt her body tingle with joy. Helena was all right. That was enough happiness to last awhile.

The studio was all Caitlin had said it was. High lights. Low lights. Cross lights. Caitlin left them, and Hunter posed Theda in her plain navy wool dress with the zipper down the back.

He switched off the lights and the setting sun came pouring in. Taking her in his arms, he simply held her for a very long time, then slowly kissed her throat and face. She melted into him hungrily and completely gave herself over to his love.

"Happy?" he whispered.

"Oh, yes. Are you?"

"Ecstatic. Now we go on with our lives. I didn't have to mention it again. Helena brought it up. She'll move tomorrow and I'll help her. She's really being good about this. I have a lot more respect for her now."

Theda wished she felt as good. She still didn't trust Helena, remembering the hatred she had seen in the woman's eyes directed at her.

Hunter took a few shots with his Polaroid, shots that mirrored her deep happiness and she took some of him. He looked like a kid on vacation in a candy store.

"Do you ever think about taking a chance on us now?" he asked her. "I know we can't have now what I hope we'll have in full later, but sometimes we have to grab what we can. I'll never press you to give more than you can give, but at least we'd be together."

Theda shook her head, took his hand and led him to a sofa where they sat down. "Sweetheart, you're deliriously happy that Helena is well after all, but you're not thinking clearly. I suffered when I lost you and when I lost Art and Kelly. They say the time for getting over grief is a year or a little more, but I'm not over mine. I went to the edge of the world and I wanted to fall off. It seems to have instilled permanent fear in me.

"And there's you, my darling. After what Helena did to you, can you truly say you trust again? And you feel you hurt her. Whatever that was, you need to face it, heal from it."

She drew a deep breath and took his hand. "And there's Curt. He's really mixed up. I suspect he knows there's little hope of your getting together with Helena again, but he feels you both love each other." She paused here, her voice low. "Do you think you might still love her?"

"No. I love you."

Looking into his eyes, she saw no sign that he spoke anything but truth.

He said thoughtfully, "My son has to learn that each person lives his own life. He simply has to accept that. In a little over four years he will be a full-grown man and knowing Curt, he will never let me or anyone stand between him and what he truly wants." He pulled her close. "I'm like that, too. And I want you. I mean to have you."

She smiled sadly. "I believe in giving a marriage every possible chance. We're not teenagers or twentysomethings anymore, but we're young enough to take time to get it all together. I have faith that you and I can heal our wounds, given time, but Curt may never come around."

He took her hand. "He'll accept us again one day. Somehow I'm sure of that." He thought it was enough that Helena was okay. He didn't intend to borrow future trouble.

"We get started tomorrow after school," he told her, rubbing her soft hands. "And now I start with my best camera, my old Nikon, but I guess Minolta has given me some of my best shots. To me, the new stuff doesn't compare." His face grew quiet, thoughtful. "I've been touted as a 'soul photographer' and I hope that's true."

And what about Hunter's soul? she thought. He was the deepest person she had ever known. His rangy, muscular body, mixed blood and Cherokee Indian skin and his sleepy black eyes always charmed her, but it was his passion and his love that took her everywhere she had ever wanted to go. She shivered a bit thinking about him, wanting to be in his arms. As if he read her mind, he leaned forward and kissed her on the mouth. "My love," he said simply.

Caitlin came back with her husband, Marty, and the twins in tow. "I hope you can use a little company," she said. "We're going out to dinner with the hellers and I wanted Theda to meet the gang."

The tall, ruddy Marty and Hunter hugged each other. "You should have gotten in touch sooner," Marty scolded Hunter.

"Yeah, I know, but things have been happening." He told them about the motorcycle accident.

Marty looked at Caitlin, smiling. "I always intended to get a Hog. They fascinate me."

Caitlin raised her eyebrows. "And let it stop at fascination. You don't get one, not as long as you have this wife and this family."

The three-year-old twins, Caleb Myles and Malinda had stood silently taking in the whole scene, deciding if they liked these two and when their minds were made up, they came forward and stared up in Hunter's and Theda's faces. Introduced themselves all over again.

Theda thought they were so precious, brown dolls with dancing brown eyes.

"I know your name," Caleb Myles said. "Mommy calls you Theda." He gazed at Theda, then at Hunter. "And your name is Hunter."

"Now, now," Caitlin said gently, "to you they're Mr. Davis and Dr. Coles."

Caleb Myles mouthed her words and repeated them. "Are you married?" he asked the two.

"Afraid not, but it's going to happen."

"Soon?" Malinda piped up.

"I hope so," Hunter told her. "We'll see that you get an invitation."

Caleb Myles's eyes lit up. "We went to a birthday party last week. It was pretty. Will your wedding be pretty?"

"Gosh, I sure hope so. As I said, you and Malinda will get invitations."

Malinda giggled. "Mommy says little kids don't go to weddings. We get— What did you say, Mommy?"

The bright eyes wanted more information and Caitlin smiled at her child. "You get restless," she said.

"I knew that," Caleb Myles bragged.

Both children went to Theda and leaned against

her knees, one on each side. She leaned down and picked up first one, then the other and put them on her lap where they looked at her with probing eyes.

"You're pretty, and you smell good," Caleb Myles said. "My mommy's pretty and she smells good, too."

Theda hugged them. They were so precious and their just-past-babyhood flesh felt wonderful in her arms. Kelly had felt like this when he was a baby. After he'd died, she'd been haunted by him in his different stages of growth, from helpless feathery baby to sturdy child to gangling teenager. She had worked with teenagers at Harney High and her heart had only been half there. She was wrong, she knew, but she had avoided true closeness with teenagers since Kelly's death—until Curt had come. Then she had opened her heart once again. Now he had fled from her.

Was she always destined to lose those she loved?

"They've made a conquest," Theda told the parents. "They're precious."

Caitlin laughed. "When they're not being devils. You know, people still talk about these kids and their terrible twos. They wrote the book." She brushed a hand across her brow. "Thank goodness that's over. I understand we get a little respite until their teens and I know we'll both get gray then...fast."

Holding the children who leaned against her, playing with her beads, Theda felt the glow of parenthood even if they weren't hers. She dreamed of babies like these with Hunter, and she wondered if they'd ever have a deeper life, let alone children. Her heart expanded and her breasts ached with longing.

And watching them, Hunter felt keen envy of what Caitlin and Marty had. He was happy that Helena was all right because it meant that Theda and he could move ahead, but to what? Both were hostage to past hurt and devastation. Hearts that could fill with passion and love could also be savaged with pain and loss. God, he thought, why did You make Your world such a mess at times? But the fantasies of Theda and him and babies, not just one, consumed him. He was sick with longing to have been with her when she carried Kelly, gave birth, raised him.

Yes, there had been happiness with Helena and Curt was still so much of his life, but there had been another son he'd never known and never would. The pain of this loss hurt like hell and he felt scalding tears behind his lids.

Sensitive to his pain, Theda kissed each child and gently set them down. They seemed a bit reluctant to go. She turned to Hunter and took his hand, squeezed. She was pretty sure she knew what was going on here as the twins went to him, climbed on his knees and snuggled on a new lap.

Caitlin grinned. "They take after Marty and the rest of the Steeles. Ever loving, ever ready to make a new conquest. They all play a game of hearts and love."

Marty shook with laughter. "And you don't?"

"Would you two be available for an invite to our community Christmas dance?" Theda asked them.

"We're always available for a dance. But I warn you, Marty will wear your feet out. Do you like South American dances?"

"Hunter does a wicked samba," Theda told her. "He's teaching me."

Marty grinned. "The samba is a wicked dance. Done wickedly, it's entrancing."

He was so droll. They were a delightful couple and Theda found herself laughing more than she had in a while.

The group left and alone, Theda and Hunter

turned to each other. "Having and raising kids is a major reason we need to move on," he said.

"I know, and believe me I'm trying. Fear is a wretched master. It takes no prisoners."

"*Au contraire,* sweetheart," he said gently. "It *makes* us prisoners. Like I've told you, I'll take a chance on us. We won't know what we can experience if we're ever free of this, but we'll have something."

"We already have something."

"We don't have a Caleb Myles and a Malinda."

"There's Curt, for you anyway. Honey, after the way Helena betrayed you, do you trust me?"

"I trust you," he answered quickly, but he'd always wanted to know about her relationship with Andre. How far had it gone? He'd always demanded exclusivity in a relationship. In the sophisticated world in which he moved, romantic musical chairs was often played, but he hadn't bought into it. Well, once, after he'd found out about Helena, but it wasn't for him. Depth was what he craved and depth was what he intended to have. But you paid a dear price for that kind of depth, he'd found. It could shatter you if it ended in betrayal.

She glanced at him obliquely. "I had lunch with Andre today. We talked about my taking over. It's been a dream. Then I think I'll put in for my own school. I think I've been running away from living my dream since the plane crash. Facing things has been hard."

He was sympathetic, but he largely heard Andre's name.

"Did you enjoy the lunch?"

"We used to do lunch all the time. Andre's a good companion. He's witty, wise, helpful."

He didn't want to hear her praise Andre. He'd never considered himself a jealous man. Was he changing?

They began getting his cameras set up. "I seldom use that camera," he said, "but I'm pulling out all the stops. I think we can finish up Saturday. I've got a seminar in Baltimore Friday night. Would you like to come along for the ride?"

"Oh, I'd love to, but Andre's putting my feet to the fire. He's giving me all sorts of assignments and I have several presentations to make. He tells me Keatha is set to make trouble if she can. You and I are both free agents and you leave my house fairly early. We have a right to a life. Helena's being with you has caused gossip, of course. A lot of people don't know you're divorced. They wonder why she's there."

"So do I, but now that she's well… I'll spend tomorrow moving her as I said. Damn the luck of having Keatha Ames living next door. I would have liked to photograph you in my studio, pose you for the photos that go on display." His eyes roved her roguishly. "Then I'd like to pose you for my eyes alone, naked and voluptuous. I'm not sure I could ever come out of you then. My God, you're sweet, Theda. Honey and ripe fruit and cream. You always were everything I've ever wanted, and hell, yes, I'll take a chance on loving you and being hurt again."

Chapter 11

Later the following afternoon, the doorbell rang as Theda cleaned up around her house. She opened the door and came face-to-face with Helena.

"Can I help you?" Theda said coolly.

Helena's smile was coldly hostile.

"I want to put my cards on the table."

Theda didn't respond, she just stepped back and led the way into her living room. She took a chair opposite Helena. She wasn't going to draw this out. "What's on your mind?" she asked.

"You're in love with Hunter," Helena said.

"Yes."

"He's been a little bit in love with you since you were both at Howard."

"What's your point?"

"You were between us the whole time we were married. Now I'm going to live between you and him."

When Theda didn't respond, Helena continued. "You hurt him terribly and I don't think he's ever really forgiven you."

Theda cleared her throat. "Has he talked about this with you?"

Helena raised her eyebrows. "He was a wreck when I got him. I saved him."

"You don't know the whole story," Theda said flatly.

"Oh, you mean, about your getting married because you were pregnant with his child…" She put a finger to her lips. "No, I'm afraid *Curt* told me that one about your son—Kelly, I believe his name was."

"I don't care to discuss this with you," Theda said.

Helena nodded. "Perhaps he *has* forgiven you, but he will never forgive himself for what he did to me."

Theda had a feeling of unease at the turn in the conversation. Hunter had alluded to a painful secret concerning Helena but he had never explained exactly what had happened.

"It was a grievous thing and I've forgiven him, but it *has* blighted my life and he knows that. He owes me and I'm damned well going to demand payment in full, *now*." Her eyes were glittering; she was a study in malevolence.

Theda felt the start of deep, burning anger. She stood up. "Is that all?" she asked with chilly politeness.

Helena gave no indication that she had been dismissed. Instead she looked around her insolently. "You've got a nice place here. No wonder Hunter spends so much time with you. I suppose he told you that I'm living with Keatha Ames since he put me out. Keatha has been very kind to me and knows you well." A small smirk lifted the corners of her mouth. Her eyes fell on the photo of Theda's late family and she moved to pick up the photo.

Theda's voice was sharp. "No, don't touch it. If that's all, I'm very busy now."

Helena really was a beautiful woman with her jet-black silk hair and creamy skin, Theda thought. But her smoky gray eyes were clear and cold. If Helena had a heart, it didn't show.

Helena stood up then. "You know the old saying that forewarned is forearmed. I want you to know what you're up against. I mean to move heaven and earth to get Hunter back and I'm not used to losing. I'm sure you'll tell him about this little visit."

"You're right, I will." Theda would be damned if she was going to wish her a pleasant evening. What she wished was that Helena would drop off the edge of the earth.

Chapter 12

"Dr. Coles, please call the principal's office," the school secretary announced over the public-address system.

Theda had just arrived on the steps of Harney High. It was seven-thirty in the morning and she frowned wondering what Andre wanted. Everything was going well. It was the third week in November. She and Hunter were ecstatic over the way his photos of her lovely back had turned out. Caitlin loved them and so did the gallery owner in New York. Theda knew she focused on this to keep her mind off what Andre wanted.

Once in Andre's office, she greeted Andre's secretary, who smiled sweetly. So far so good, she thought.

She found Andre pacing like a man possessed. A large manila envelope lay on the table by his desk. He picked it up and held it out to her.

"Good morning," he said brusquely. "Brace yourself for a shock."

She blinked a bit. "What *is* it?"

He picked up the envelope as if it were a snake and pulled out a photograph. Theda felt the breath knocked from her as he turned the paper over and she saw her naked back from the hips up.

"Oh, my God!" she whispered. "Where did you get this?"

He looked at her narrowly. "My housekeeper said it came yesterday, special delivery. I started to call you last night, but I wanted to think this over. It is you."

He sounded accusatory, and she flinched, but she willed herself to be calm. "This photo has to have been heavily altered. I was wearing a back-less ball gown. I was *not* naked."

He passed the back of his hand over his forehead. "Please sit down," he said.

Theda found her legs shaking and cobwebs seemed to cloud her brain. They sat side by side in tub chairs and he reached over and pressed her hand. "I believe you, but who would do such a thing?"

She drew a deep breath. "I'm sure this photo can be checked for tampering. It will take time, but it can be done. We'll see that it's done."

He shook his head. "Did you get a copy in the mail?"

"No."

"Lord, I wonder who else it went to. And who sent it?"

Theda was pretty sure she knew where it came from. Who else but Helena and her cohort Keatha would do such a thing?

She told Andre what she thought and he nodded. "It certainly seems possible, but we could never prove that in a thousand years."

"At least we can prove the tampering. And we know that Helena had the only likely access and opportunity.'

"That's a start." Andre got up and began pacing again. He stopped for a moment, looked over at Theda and sighed.

"I'm so sorry," he said.

"So am I," she found herself whispering. She was so angry she felt nauseated.

"I wish I knew who else had these. Well, I guess we'll find out soon enough."

He was cut off by a booming voice from the outer office. After a moment, Reverend Whisonant was ushered in to the principal's office. He was carrying a brown envelope.

"Good morning, you two. Ah, Dr. Coles, just the woman I was looking for. I hate to be the bearer of bad news, but did you receive one of these?" He gestured to the envelope in his hand.

"We were just wondering who else got the photos," Andre said.

Reverend Whisonant rubbed his chin. "Since I got it, we can assume all the school board members got one. It may have been distributed over the entire community, although I think it will serve the necessary purpose for just the school board to receive it. And you, Andre, received one. Theda, did you?"

She shook her head no.

"It's the devil's own handiwork," Reverend Whisonant said. "You and your late husband were so popular in this community. Work with children, with the poor, mentoring. You both did it all and Kelly made friends by the dozen. You have quite a legacy here. You're a model church member. I admire you as much as I've admired any human in my life. Know that I am with you all the way."

"I thank you," Theda told him with tears choking her.

He smiled. "Don't thank me. Thank the Lord for making you the wonderful person you are." He cleared his throat. "I understand that Mr. Davis's ex-wife is in town. Might she have anything to do with this?"

Theda told him what Andre and she had discussed and he pursed his mouth. "This is quite a mess." He looked at her hands. "Are you and Davis engaged, or planning on becoming engaged?"

She thought a moment before she responded. "No, we're not," she said finally.

"Ah," Reverend Whisonant said, "then what we must do now is damage control. How long will it take to prove that the photo is not real?"

"We have the originals. I have to talk with Hunter about this. It's so unexpected. We could rush it through a photo lab. He has many friends who own special labs. He can do the initial checking, testing. He can prove in a heartbeat that it was altered."

"Good. Good. Now…"

A shrill female voice came in to them, a woman demanding to see Andre immediately. Again, Andre's buzzer sounded and Keatha burst through, sputtering as she entered.

"Well, at least you've apprehended the miscreant."

"And good morning to you, Mrs. Ames," Reverend Whisonant said pleasantly.

Keatha glared at Reverend Whisonant. "Of course you're on her side. If she murdered half the community, you'd be on her side."

Reverend Whisonant raised his eyebrows. I'd say she'd be the least likely to do anything wrong. There are others far more culpable."

"Explain this photo, missy," Keatha demanded as she looked daggers at Theda.

Looking at Keatha, Theda felt that the woman had everything to do with this, even if she had not done the actual deed.

Willing herself to calmness, Theda explained what had happened, that the photo had been altered and Keatha snorted. "A likely story. Think

I was born yesterday?" Her gaze swept the men. "Are you two buying that? Oh, I know I'm older now and my power with men is gone. But why be fools and believe anything you're told by a woman who can't keep her clothes on?"

Keatha meant several things by her remark and they all knew it. The men could barely suppress a smile, but Theda felt livid at the attack.

The older woman moved in for the kill. "Mrs. Davis, yes, she still claims his name..."

"They are divorced," Theda pointed out. "She left him for another man."

"But she wants him back and from what I can see he wants her. You're not around all the time, missy, although you're there enough."

"I'm not there that often."

"Probably because he makes excuses to keep you away so she won't be jealous. He still cares for Helena, believe me. I can see it in both of them."

Theda saw no need to say that Hunter wanted her, Theda, over all the time and forbade Helena to come over while she was there.

"Well, we dawdle, talking as the kids say *trash* when school board business is what we're about. Did you get a photo, Mrs. Ames?" Reverend Whisonant's face was stern.

"You bet I got this sinful thing," Keatha stormed, reaching into her tote bag and bringing out an envelope. "Special delivery late yesterday." She nodded at Andre. "I'd have called you if I'd received it earlier." She looked at Reverend Whisonant. "Three of the key players are in this room and we can get the ball rolling. I say you withdraw your name to be acting principal and you do it now!"

Reverend Whisonant raised his hand. "Please, Mrs. Ames. As president of the school board I will call an emergency meeting tonight and we'll discuss this."

"Discuss, hump-p-ph. I don't see that there's anything to discuss. And don't you forget that I'm treasurer of that same school board and I carry a lot of weight."

"I'm forgetting nothing," Reverend Whisonant said drolly. "Perhaps you've forgotten the Christian edict that we judge not that we be not judged. I must go now, but there will be a meeting at city hall at eight o'clock. I want both of you to attend," he said to Theda and Andre.

Keatha wasn't backing down easily. She looked at Theda with narrowed eyes. "A woman who's no more moral than she has to be always brings trouble in her wake."

* * *

Back in her office Theda found Angela waiting for her, a manila envelope clutched nervously in her hand. "I saw you going into Andre's office. You've seen this then." She thrust the photo at Theda.

"I've seen it. I don't think I have to tell you what happened."

Angela's face was troubled. "Honey, Hunter is an *artist.* It's okay if you take nude pictures. It's just that we're so backward in Crystal Lake. I'm sure the artistic community in D.C. would think nothing of it."

"Angela. Those photos were altered. I posed in a ball gown with a very low back."

Angela's eyes went wide. "But who would…" she began. "Helena?"

"Please don't leave out Keatha Ames."

They sat at a table. Angela pressed Theda's hand. "You know I'm always with you all the way. If Ken wouldn't kill me, I'd pose butt-naked for a great photographer like Hunter."

Theda couldn't help laughing, then she sobered. "I guess there goes my job. I'll never get a chance to properly explain this."

"But you've been tops with the school board and you earned it."

"Public sentiment can change so quickly. I wonder if the whole community got this drivel?"

"Quite a bill if they did. Mine came special delivery."

"Keatha has money," Theda said. "Lies and intrigue fill some people's lives."

"Amen, sister!" Angela bolstered her. "How did she get hold of the photos?"

"Hunter took just scads of them. I'm sure some of them went into the trash. Keatha's house is next door. She could have watched for them. Curt said he told Helena I was posing. I'm sure she was curious, especially when we moved to a studio in D.C."

"I love intrigue, but not when it hurts someone I love. Did you get a photo in the mail?"

"No. I'm going to call Hunter now and see if he got one. On second thought, he'd have called me if he had."

Angela stood up. "I have to check out now. Call me if you need anything or just want to talk. Honey, you're such a good person. I predict you'll win this. People know who you are."

But Theda could have cried. It was all coming down on her now. Her spirits had been high at first. Now reality was setting in. She knew and loved Crystal Lake, had lived here all her life.

Did she have enough friends here and would they unite behind her?

Her cell phone rang. Hunter. His voice was somber, rushed. "Honey, you're going to be shocked and I'm sorry, but I got a photo in the mail this morning, special delivery. Theda, the shots I made of you have been altered to look as if you posed nude…."

She told him then about Andre's call and the meeting in Andre's office. He was silent a long moment. "Damn it to hell! I wonder how many people those mailings have gone to. Baby, I'm coming over now."

She shook her head vehemently. "I'm not sure that's a good idea."

"You need me now and I'm coming."

He hung up and she looked up to find Kitty standing by the windows. She had been unaware of her coming in. Kitty came to her quickly. "We got a photo in the mail yesterday," she began. "Dr. Coles, what is somebody trying to do to you?"

Somehow Kitty's words affected her more deeply than anyone's and she felt scalding tears just behind her eyelids. The girl came to her and put her arms around her. "My mom is furious. She started to call you, but she wanted to give you a chance to sort it out. If we got it, it's a cinch many others did, too. My mom said to tell you she'll be calling and that we're a thousand percent behind you. She said she's been deeply in love and she knows what can happen."

Kitty hugged her tightly. "Now, anything you want me to do, you just tell me. I can get an excuse from class. Will you be all right?"

Theda patted the girl's hand. "I'll be all right. I really *will* be all right."

Hunter strode along the corridor of Harney's downstairs hall as classes were changing, his face like a thundercloud.

Theda sat at a table with her back to the door of her office. Hunter thought she looked dejected. He went to her, pulled her up and hugged her. She forced a small laugh. "We're the subjects of enough gossip, sweetheart. All I need to hear is that we were making love in the middle of my office."

He hugged her again. "Baby, I'm *so* sorry I got you into this."

"Who, Hunter? Who *sent* them? Helena?"

"Possibly. With Keatha's help, probably. I haven't known Helena to be vicious. You've told me Keatha can be."

They sat down then at the table. "I want to kiss you so bad, stroke you, make you feel better. You look like you've lost your best friend."

He took her hand and pressed it hard. "We need to be together tonight."

"There's a school board meeting scheduled at eight o'clock tonight. Lord, I'm dreading this."

"I'll be there with you."

"Maybe you shouldn't."

"Nonsense. I'll *take* you."

"Honey, I can't begin to tell you how much this hurts me. I know how long you've had your heart set on being a school principal and now was the beginning of your chance to get a major school. You dream high and you hurt hard when you fail. Can you forgive me?"

Her eyes misted with tears then. "Forgive you for loving me? For using your artistic gifts to my glory? Hunter, the photos of me are splendid, art at its greatest. How can I be angry with you when I love you, and I'm grateful to you for immortalizing me?"

He kissed her hand and neither knew that Keatha stood just outside the door.

Chapter 13

Hunter stood in Theda's living room, nervously waiting to take her to the special school board meeting. He retraced his thoughts from the time he wanted to photograph her gorgeous back. Why hadn't he waited? But what *would* have been a good time? He drew a deep breath. He had spent too much time in parts of Europe where this uproar would have been considered foolish. He had a masterpiece and he sure as hell wasn't going to be ashamed of it, but what about Theda's future? It mattered to him more than his own.

"Hunter?"

He had been lost in thought. He turned and his heart hurt with her loveliness. He had asked her to put on her yellow diamond ring and she had dressed to match with a pale yellow wool dress with a boat neckline and cream pearl drop earrings. He felt she looked so vulnerable.

"Come here," he told her.

She slowly came to him and he took her in his arms and simply held her for a while. "I'm so sorry," he said.

She put a finger to his lips. "Don't say that again. Neither of us has anything to be sorry for. We've done nothing wrong."

He kissed her then, long and thoroughly, savoring the feel, the smell, the taste of her. His tongue went deep into the precious hollows of her mouth and he took pure honey that rocketed thrills through his muscular body.

"Are you scared?" he asked her.

"A little."

"Don't be. I'll take care of you."

Every board member was in attendance at the meeting. Keatha looked smug. Tonight she was in her element, and she sat with her eyes half-closed as Hunter and Theda walked in.

Andre smiled at the couple when they walked in.

Reverend Whisonant's eyes lit up when his glance lingered on Theda with deep approval. This was a sticky business and he regretted this awful photograph incident.

The room was arranged so that comfortable chairs were lined up facing a blackboard and an easel. Narrow tables had been placed in front of the chairs. Theda and Hunter sat to the right of the group in chairs with tables before them. Hunter glanced supportively at Theda often and his heart hurt with wanting to comfort her. The more he thought about it, the more he knew that what he planned to do tonight after the meeting was right for them.

All eyes were on the two people concerned. Reverend Whisonant began with a prayer: "God, tonight, we are gathered here to consider one of our fellow humans. I ask only that we judge not, that we be not judged. Fill our hearts with compassion, with love and forgiveness. And let him who is without sin cast the first stone...."

The room was very quiet when he finished and Keatha looked down, a bit less smug.

Reverend Whisonant stood silently for a long

while before he said, "We all have the photographs. I have made a survey of the community. All school board members got them, all Harney teachers…"

"I brought mine." Without further ado, Keatha pulled her photo from the envelope and held it up. The five men on the board half smiled. Keatha and her two allies looked properly disapproving. The other four women's visages were unreadable. Keatha put the photo faceup on her table, looking triumphantly around her. At last, the hussy would get what she deserved.

The chair recognized Keatha and she began indignantly. "I will not waste your time nor mine with pretty words. We are a highly moral community here in Crystal Lake. We are not the fleshpots of Europe, or New York or New Orleans, although I pray for that tormented city now. Dr. Coles is to replace Dr. Lord while he is on sabbatical. Then I understand she will take a school of her own." She smirked then. "Scandal is always unfortunate, but it seldom happens when we exercise the care we must take as women." She cleared her throat. "My late, beloved mother always said a man can do no more than a woman lets him do."

"Amen!" one of Keatha's minions said.

Keatha blushed. "Now, Mr. Davis, the photographer who took these photographs, lives next door to me and I love him the way I love my own son, Mort." At the mention of Mort's name, she shot a malevolent glance at Theda and continued. "Mr. Davis's wife lives with me and has become a treasured friend—"

"I believe she's his *ex*-wife," Reverend Whisonant cut in.

"Yes, well," Keatha simpered, "I guess I'm from the old school that believes that once married, always married. I know for a fact she wants him back and from the way they look at each other, he wants *her* back. They have a wonderful son between them and he would move heaven and earth to have them together again. But I digress. The photograph in question." Here she held up the photo and sighed. "As I said, we are a moral place. This is art and a man I revere took this photo." Her voice got hard then. "But Dr. Coles posed for it *in the nude.*" Her voice raked Theda as she emphasized the last three words. "Is this the kind of judgment she will use training our sons and daughters to be upstanding men and women?"

She sat down, certain her arrows had struck home.

Reverend Whisonant stood up. "I felt it would help us to have Mr. Hunter Davis explain what has happened here. It will be almost impossible to prove who did this, but God knows and in all our hearts, vengeance is His. Mr. Davis."

Hunter pressed Theda's hand and stood, walked over to stand in front of the group. "I've taken many photographs in my life," he began, "but none has pleased me more than the photograph in question. It's a photograph of my dearly beloved, Dr. Theda Coles." A small ripple of shock ran among the group.

Hunter continued. "The past is *not* prologue here for Dr. Coles and I will be married at some point soon." His eyes met Theda's and held. "This woman is the love of my life and if there is any fault here, it's wholly mine and I take full blame. My masterpiece—and, yes, it's the best I've ever done—my masterpiece was *altered*. Dr. Coles was fully clad in a backless ball gown when the photo was taken."

A sustained gasp went the length of the room and all eyes went to Hunter, then Theda.

"But how?" a woman began, and as Hunter began to answer, one of Keatha's minions spoke up.

"Oh, that's easy enough to say, but can you prove it?"

"I can and I will. I did my own developing on this one and my imprints are all there. When a photo is altered or retouched, patterns are left where the changes were made. I took the offending photo that I received in the mail to a photo lab and they will give me a report in a few days. Meantime, I can easily see what happened. I will see that Reverend Whisonant gets that report."

"Hold on, sir," the woman who had asked for proof demanded. "Everybody brags that you're world famous, so you have clout. Couldn't you pay a lab owner you know to certify that the photo you made was, I believe you used the term *altered?*"

Hunter shrugged. "Ma'am, you're free to choose a lab that you trust."

"I favor that."

Hunter nodded. "I can supply you with a list of photo labs, or you can go to any reputable camera shop and they'll supply you with such a list."

Reverend Whisonant frowned. "What is the shortest possible time this can be done? I want this over as soon as is humanly possible. This is a terrible, painful affair and a woman's reputation is at stake. Time is of the essence."

"I'd say no more than two days," Hunter said.

The board decided that Reverend Whisonant would contact a camera store and get a list, contact a lab and abide by their report.

Reverend Whisonant took the floor then. "I'm certain this will be resolved in favor of Dr. Coles. As soon as we have the report we will give our recommendation to a joint meeting of the community and school board. We're honored to have a man like Mr. Davis in our community and no less honored to have Dr. Coles training our children.

"A grave and criminal injustice has been done here. Let us rectify it and be at peace with ourselves. I move that we adjourn."

Keatha could hardly wait to get home where Helena waited for her. Keatha felt ecstatic. Hunter was going to sing a different tune when his lover was fired, and she had no doubt at all that she *would* be fired. Altered? Retouched? Very well, but who would pay any attention to that. Enough people had seen the nude photo and it was engraved on their minds. They wouldn't forget. This was Crystal Lake, not New York City or even D.C.

Helena had gone outside to smoke several cigarettes. Keatha wouldn't like it if she knew she smoked so she always waited until Keatha was away. She had just gotten back inside and sucked on a breath mint when the front door slammed.

Keatha threw her purse and tote on the sofa and hugged Helena.

"Well, I've done what had to be done and I did it well," she exulted. "I've wanted to shoot that tramp's hide down and she's given me the ammunition. I always knew she was a strumpet." She sighed and put a hand to her breast. Her laughter then was coldly evil. "My dear, all you have to do now is to pick up the pieces."

"Where are we going?" Theda turned sideways and tucked one leg under her as the car motor purred.

"You ask too many questions. Special place. Special action."

"Oh, you." They had both been silent since coming out of the meeting. Now she asked, "What did you think?"

"It wasn't too bad. They seemed surprised about the photo being altered. We haven't talked about this much, but Keatha is my main candidate for the culprit."

"What about Helena? She's the one who has access to your house." Was her voice a little shrill? she wondered. And was he protecting Helena?

"If she went to my studio, Curt would tell me and I don't think he'd let her. He knows I don't want her there."

What Theda thought was that Curt was putty in his mother's hands. If she wanted to go to the moon and he had a plane with enough altitude, he'd take her. "Has he told you she's asked questions about what we're doing? Curt knows you're taking shots of me that will go on display in a gallery."

"Yeah, he told me she asked a few questions. Helena's wrapped up in her own little world. She's selfish, not evil. She might very well know about the plot, but I doubt she had much to do with it."

Theda was adamant. "I'm not sure. I think you underrate how much she wants you back."

Smiling, he turned to look at her for a few seconds. "Too late. I'm spoken for."

The big car took the miles easily and soon they had traversed the beltway and Maryland town signs were coming into view.

"I've got to know where we're going."

"No, you don't. Not until we get there. I've got a surprise for you."

"You're full of wonderful surprises."

"I think this will set things right."

He sounded mysterious and she was intrigued. She switched on the stereo and got a late-night classical station. Such music always soothed her and she needed that tonight. Hunter's arms could soothe her, too, and her body ached for him to be inside her. He put a hand on her thigh. "How're you holding up?"

"Mostly I'm just wondering what *you're* up to."

"Rest," he said softly. "Everything's going to be A-okay."

She lay back and listened to the melody from Dvořák's *Eighth Symphony* and wished it lasted longer. The rest of the symphony was superb, but it was that melody that haunted her.

"We're going to get back really late," he said. "You'll be sleepy tomorrow, and I'll be happy tomorrow."

Now she was really intrigued, but she kept quiet.

It seemed a long time before they went through country territory, then into a brightly lit town that seemed curiously alive at this time of the night. She saw the welcoming sign that heralded Medville, Maryland. Haven for Lovers.

"Let's move here," she teased him. "I like what they stand for."

"We could live in hell and it would be heaven."

"You're so sweet."

"Feel better?"

"I'm with you. That always helps."

"You'll feel even better soon."

They passed the pastel buildings and from the lit signs she got it. "This is the town where people get married with no waiting time."

"Yep." He pulled into a large parking lot with few cars, parked and pushed both seats back.

"What on earth?"

He shifted and got down on his knees with a small navy leather jeweler's box in his hand. Snapping it open, she gasped at the glitter of the yellow diamond wedding band in the streetlight. It matched the yellow diamond she wore.

"I'm going to dispense with the lengthy proposal," he told her huskily. "I love you. I want you. I need you. Be my wife and love me forever, the way I do and will love you. And this way you don't have to worry about the gossip or Harney's school board."

For a long while she was choked with tears and her heart pounded. "My darling," she finally whispered. She put a hand on the back of his head, bent and kissed him long and hard. "We can't be married just now."

"I don't take rejection easily, not from someone I love the way I love you."

"Sweetheart, sit up. We've got to talk."

"Let's get married first. Then we'll make world-class love. *Then* we'll talk, all you want to."

It was the hardest thing she'd ever had to say and she was heartsick. He sat back on the seat and turned to her. "Well."

"There's Curt," she said. "He would be devastated."

"I've told you and I've told Curt that each person has a life to live and no one can live it for him or her."

"He's going through the most difficult period of his life. Don't make it harder for him. Next year this time he'll be in college and better able to handle this. He'll be away from both of you and it will be easier."

"I don't agree."

"Then there's Helena," she said.

"What about Helena? She's history."

"No, I don't think she is."

"I loved Helena, but she left me for another man…."

"And you can't forgive her. You're still angry." She sighed deeply then. "Hunter, don't you see, you don't get as angry with someone as you are with Helena unless a part of you still cares for her?"

It was his turn to sigh. "They say we hate the ones *we* hurt more than the ones who hurt *us.* There's a lot of truth in that."

"What *is* this hurt you dealt Helena? Maybe you're seeing more in it than is there."

He shook his head. "I ruined her life. Believe me, she feels it. She *will* feel it as long as she lives."

"Won't you tell me what you did to her?"

"I talked it over with a psychologist when I couldn't stand it anymore. I've gone on with my life and tried to forgive myself. Perhaps in time... I'll will tell you at some point. Right now it sticks in my throat like bile. Trust me. It's ugly."

"I could forgive you anything." She hugged him then and felt his hard, muscular body pressing her tender curves. "Try me."

"Please wait a little while."

Her heart was thudding with anxiety and with need. He wanted to protect her and she was grateful, but she was certain they shouldn't marry. Tears of anguish rose in her throat. Her voice was low as she told him, "There's *me,* Hunter. Fear of heartbreak has frozen my heart. I can only hope that someday I'll be free of this crippling fear, but right now, I'm shackled to it."

He crushed her to him, buried his face in her hair. "My darling. My darling," he whispered.

Her body flamed with raging heat then, desire sweeping every cell of her. Liquid gold filled her veins. This man had her body, heart and soul and it was never going to be different. "I want you inside me," she whispered. "Let's go home and make love."

His desire matched hers, he thought. Fire raced along his entire system and the need to possess her possessed him. But he stroked her back as he told her, "No, love, right now you need soothing and comforting and I'm going to do that for you. I love you too much to ever take advantage of you."

"You wouldn't be taking advantage of me. Don't you want me?"

"You know damned well I do. I could take you here and now and be happy, but your reputation has already suffered enough. Forgive me for even kissing you the way I'm going to do now."

His lips on her throat were tender at first, pulling back the neckline of her dress and tonguing the soft flesh. She shuddered in ecstasy. They were in a public place and this mustn't last long. He took her face in his hands and kneaded her jawline, playing with her face with his tongue.

"What are you trying to do to me?" she whispered.

"Make you mine."

"That's double jeopardy. I'm already yours."

His index finger went over her lips. "Be quiet and kiss me back."

She did as he asked in spades as electrical charges shot through them both. She was sick with wanting him and she caught his tongue with her own and sucked it.

Waves of fever went through him as he returned the favor and worked her tongue with his. Inside the car was warm and both had removed their coats, so he felt the lushness of her body and it set him on fire. He kissed her throat again all over with tiny nibbling kisses that drove her wild.

"I don't need soothing and comfort," she murmured, "I need *you* inside me."

But every instinct in him said he shouldn't take her tonight. She needed assurance that he loved her and forgoing this heavenly pleasure was the best way he knew to make her know that he loved her for herself, not her body, and that he would do anything to protect her.

Drawing a bit away he told her, "I've hurt you and I've hurt Helena…"

She put a finger to his lips. "Let's don't talk about Helena."

"We're going to have to go. You've got school tomorrow."

She smiled a bit now. "I've got you tonight. Thank you, sweetheart, for making me feel so much better. And please, the photos you took are too gorgeous for any kind of regret. When we're old, we'll still treasure them."

"We have a lot of memories, past, present and future. I feel so blessed to have you, Theda, in my heart and in my life. Right now I wish we could go away, just the two of us and be alone for a while. Someone called today to say I've been chosen as Photographer of the Year by the Photographic Society of America. They're holding the convention in New Orleans in January. Will you go with me?"

She hugged him again, felt the flames again. "You know I will."

He smiled a bit then, said wistfully, "When we *do* make love, I'm going to make you weep with joy. Give you everything I've got and then some."

"Um-m-m. Trouble is, I want it *now*…."

Chapter 14

The next night, there was something Curt had to do and he dreaded it, confronting Helena, but he did it and he faced her now at Keatha's house. Keatha wasn't home. She was all over the community drumming up support to get Theda kicked out. That photo of Dr. Coles was tearing him up. At his tender age, he had the soul of an artist; the naked body was sacrosanct to him. And she hadn't been naked. He had seen all the negatives, had developed some of them and he thought them stunning.

Helena looked at her son lovingly. "You wanted to talk to me, honey. Are you upset by the photos your dad took of his lady love?"

She sounded catty and he hated catty women.

"Mom, the day you asked me to go to the drugstore for you…"

She frowned a moment. "Oh, yes, what about it?"

"You didn't go up to Dad's studio by any chance, did you? While I was gone?"

Her eyes went wide. "Honey, I had a headache that day. If I'd tried to go up those stairs, I'd have fallen down."

Why didn't he believe her?

"Now," she said, "let's get back to basics. I'll bet the school is in an uproar. Little Miss Niceness caught in the buff."

"It wasn't like that, Mom. Those pictures were altered. But if she *had* posed, it's okay. Nudity is a part of art. Spain's great artist Goya could tell you that, and so many others."

"Oh, you've grown up, haven't you? Well, I'll tell you this. I don't want a woman who poses in the nude as guidance counselor at my son's school."

He raised his voice then, wholly exasperated with her. "It wasn't the way you keep telling it. Dr. Coles is a good person…."

Helena sounded aggrieved then. "Am I losing you to her, too? Honey, please help us to be a family again."

He nodded, so mixed-up he couldn't think.

"Stay and talk with me awhile," she said, patting the sofa beside her.

"I gotta go," he said, feeling sick at heart.

Once at home, Curt couldn't stop thinking about his beautiful mother and how much he still needed her. Dad would be happy with them again. He truly felt that. She was a woman Curt had always worshipped. How could his dad want another woman?

But a part of him knew that Helena had taken the photo or photos and that was wrong. He glanced down at the expensive watch she'd given him for his birthday. She'd always lavished presents on him and he'd always loved what she'd given him. Presents often more suitable for the man he'd become than for the boy he was.

Love for his mother filled his heart and he said a silent prayer for a resolution to this mess. The problem was his father wasn't helping things. Was it true what the boys said, that a girl or woman you slept with could lead you around by the nose?

His dad was with Dr. Coles so much, he was sure they were lovers. Sometimes he even envisioned what they did. How sick was that? he thought.

Chapter 15

It was early the next week before the school board-community meeting took place in Crystal Lake's city hall auditorium. Reverend Whisonant looked out over the sizable group and his eyes fell on Theda and Hunter. They were sitting together.

Clearing his throat, he began; "Ladies and gentlemen. We're here tonight to discuss an ugly incident in our community."

Looking out on the audience, his eyes fell on Keatha and two of her school board cronies. She looked smug and self-satisfied. He thought of a cat with a canary in its mouth and anger filled him. He had no doubt that Keatha was behind this.

Reverend Whisonant continued. "I'll explain further what the meeting is about. I've talked with small groups all over the community, passed out written statements refuting these infamous lies. Dr. Coles has lived among us all her life. She has worked at Harney High many years and is now a guidance counselor there. As you know, she aspires to fill Dr. Lord's spot as principal when he goes on sabbatical next year."

He went on to explain the background of what had happened.

"Ladies and gentlemen, we've taken the offending photo to a major photography chain and they've given us a written report that the photos were, indeed, altered."

After a few more comments, Reverend Whisonant threw the floor open for comments.

The questions began.

The first question was from the woman in the front row. "Like so many of you, I love Dr. Coles and she *must* stay with us and be our principal while Dr. Lord is away. I will vote for her and I beg her other friends to do the same."

When the woman sat down, a smattering of

applause sounded and Reverend Whisonant shushed them, half smiling.

An incensed Keatha stood up then, her mind on a rumble. She forced herself to be somber, but she was rejoicing inside because she still had one ace up her sleeve.

It was so long before Keatha began to speak papers rustled and people whispered. She tried to emulate Reverend Whisonant's magnificent presence but fell flat. "I want no pornographic claptrap in a school that my wonderful son graduated from," she began. "And these photos are p-o-r-n, pure and simple. Now, it has been said that the pictures have been altered. I don't believe it. Many things could have happened..." But she recounted none of them. "I say we do not need a woman of this caliber as principal. Dr. Theda Coles hides her evil behind a mantle of goodness. I say it's time for her to pay for her evil deeds.

"Hunter Davis is as dear to me as my own son and I'm trying to put him back together with his wife. Because, you see, I happen to think from the way they look at each other, they still love each other.

"The *Bible* speaks of strange women, *wicked* women and in my opinion Theda Coles is such a woman. I think we should see that she never takes over for our beloved Dr. Andre Lord. Thank you."

She was puffed, proud and sure of herself. "Vote her out, my friends. *We can do far better!*"

There was a sprinkling of applause when she finished and sat down and the two women who sat with her clapped enthusiastically.

A stalwart young man stood up then. He looked dour and unforgiving. "I don't agree with the good Reverend," he said. "I think it is our business to judge what most affects us. I'm casting no stones, but I do have a small pebble in my hand." A few people tittered.

"I agree with Mrs. Ames that we need no pornography in our community. Our children are at risk and I think most of the entertainment our children are subjected to should be wiped off the face of the earth."

The man's voice rose here and like Keatha, he seemed to be competing with Reverend Whisonant for effect. "We cannot always win, but we can always fight," the man went on. "Protect our children from this filth. If you ask me, even a backless evening gown is distasteful. What was this woman thinking? And what did the man who took the photo think of *her?* This is not the kind of thing I can respect. We need to keep this kind of filth out of Crystal Lake."

Again a smattering of applause. Reverend Whisonant held up his hand. "There are many who wish to speak, so I ask that you please be brief. And the floor is open for questions and comments, not oratory. Let us continue."

A woman stood to speak. She smiled at Theda. "I want to say that I am one of your biggest admirers, Dr. Coles. You've been a real honor to this community. I notice that you didn't speak on your own behalf tonight and I wonder if there are a few words you'd like to say. Believe me, I understand if you wish to say nothing at all."

Theda's heart raced. Glancing at Hunter who pressed her hand, she stood and began to speak in a strong clear voice.

"I want to say at the outset that I love this city and this community. I have had successes and I have had failures. I hope I have taken both in stride." She paused.

"We live on the edge of a metropolis, Washington, D.C., a world-class city. A backless gown is just that. No more. When Hunter spoke to me about taking the photograph, I saw and see nothing wrong with it and we went ahead."

She paused again, then said sadly, "I think this is one of the best examples of a photographer's art. But something went grievously wrong. Some mean-spirited person saw fit to alter the photograph, make it appear that I posed in the nude, which I did not." She wondered then if she should say it, but she had to say, "I love this man and I believe in him as I think he believes in me.

"All I ask is that you make every effort to judge me *fairly*. I'm human, as weak and as strong as you are. And I *do* trust your judgment. Thank you."

The room was quiet when Theda finished. She sat down and Hunter felt his heart burst with love for her. He took and squeezed her hand and held it a minute.

There was a rustle and a vivid stir when Andre stood and was recognized. He sat on a front seat, stood up and faced the audience, was silent for a moment, frowning. "It saddens me to be here on this occasion," he began. "Dr. Coles is not only a valued coworker, but a treasured friend. It has been my hope that she will replace me for the time I'm on sabbatical."

The audience held its breath as he spoke.

"Dr. Coles has been done a vicious disservice,"

Andre said. "Put yourself in her place. It could happen to any one of you at any time. We live in an age of marvelous possibilities, but some of those possibilities can turn ugly and even dangerous as they did for Dr. Coles. Please don't let monsters succeed in wrecking a life. Dr. Coles is innocent. Ladies and gentlemen, I implore you to give her your vote of confidence as she has always given you hers. Give her your love as she has always given you her love."

His speech was effective and applause burst around him. Like Reverend Whisonant, this was a man they honored and revered.

Both Angela and her husband, Ken, spoke and were well received, as was Mrs. Sanders. Theda listened to them as they extolled her virtues and it felt wonderful to have friends like them.

Suddenly from the back Helena stood up, was recognized and swiftly walked to the front, not six feet away from where Theda and Hunter sat.

Gone was the glamour. Dressed in a black suit, Helena looked every inch the small-town matron. Her voice was strong, clear. "Many will think me an interloper," she said, "but I have a dearly beloved son at Harney. My son is also Hunter Davis's son," Helena said.

"I don't consider it decent to have a woman posing in the nude and leading my son…"

Hunter's head jerked up. *Was Helena losing her mind?* The whole meeting had been a refutation that Theda had posed in the nude. Didn't Helena see how stupid she sounded? But he thought then that there was a method to her madness. The old adage: tell a big enough lie and many people will believe it. And Helena was now embellishing the lie.

"I will not keep you longer because you will want to vote, but I beg you to vote with your hearts. I want my son and your kids to be safe from pornographic concepts. Vote with your hearts as I will vote with mine. Thank you."

All eyes were on Helena as she walked slowly to the back of the auditorium and sat down.

The audience was quiet for a moment, then grew restive. Reverend Whisonant rightly assumed that they were ready to vote.

As the voting began, Theda turned to Hunter, and said, "I can't stay here. I'm too nervous. Andre will call me with the results."

"Okay," he said, his heart going out to her, "I'll take you home."

* * *

At Theda's, Hunter and she drank hot chocolate laced with fine brandy and whipped cream. "Hunter, what do you think the outcome will be?"

"I think you'll win," he said without hesitation.

He set his cup on the coffee table, then took hers and set it down, took her in his arms.

He kissed her fervently at first, then held back.

"I should be going. No point in adding fuel to the fire." He mocked Keatha. "'He was there until the wee hours of the morning. And right in the middle of this mess. They have no shame.'"

Theda laughed at his falsetto. "She'd be right, you know. I *have* no shame where you're concerned. But since you're here, we might as well take advantage of the situation." Her soft hands stroked him as she patterned tiny kisses over his leathery face and muscular neck. She was turning on higher by the minute and she wanted to stay that way. Anxiety filled her and she sought release from it in him.

He knew exactly how she felt. He wanted to protect her from further gossip, but he wanted to comfort her. She was making it so easy for him to stay. Her floral perfume and her body that was growing warmer by the minute enticed him.

With a flirtatious smile, she straddled his lap, pressed down and wriggled. His erection was enormous. He buried his face in the hollows of her throat and peppered her with sudden, wicked kisses that thrilled her to the marrow of her bones. How long had it been since they'd made love? she wondered hazily. Too long.

There was no time for foreplay as they tore off each other's clothes. Her softly firm buns pressing down on him hard were warm, and her breasts against his face were making him delirious with lust. He suckled them hungrily, then eased as he licked each one voluptuously.

"Stay the night," she whispered. "If they don't give me the position, I'll need you here."

"Baby, don't. I think you will win the vote. They know a good woman when they see one."

"Then please stay until Andre calls and tells me what happened."

"All right," he said.

"You'll stay then?"

"Just until Andre calls, and listen, sweetheart, I don't want to be making love when the call comes. I don't like interruptions."

"We have a while. They've got to count the votes." She threw back her head and completely let herself go. "Don't talk so much. Make wild, crazy love to me."

He eased her up a little from his lap, slipped off his pants and her panties. Then he slipped his greatly swollen, throbbing penis inside her, groaning at the blazing heat of her inner walls and the honeyed wetness of her. He saw her through a haze and she was more than beautiful.

She took his bottom lip and sucked it as he gripped her buns and massaged them feverishly. Then he took her face in his hands and blotted out all reality for her. He gripped her waist and they both came explosively with heat so intense it seemed surreal.

She relaxed against him then, feeling his strength and his love, and he held her in the warm circle of his arms, still nuzzling her neck. He shook his head then, thrilling at the vivid sensations of him throbbing and her rhythmically holding him in and letting him go.

He looked at her, smiling sleepily. "Like what you got?"

"*Loved* what I got. I want more of the same."

"Lady, you're a hard taskmaster."

"You shouldn't make it so good."

* * *

It was ll:45 p.m. when the call came and Theda picked up the phone.

"You're safe," Andre said huskily, "and I congratulate you. I'm really happy for you. The vote was three hundred twenty to eighty-four."

Theda felt relief wash over her in waves. "Andre, thank you so much for speaking out for me. I'll be in tomorrow morning to see you."

Theda tongue-kissed Hunter's slightly hairy chest and rolled her face from side to side on it. "I'm not letting you go. I know a good thing when I see it."

"Nothing doing, honey. I'm going to protect you from here on, from myself and the outside world. Starting tomorrow, I'm going to give you the life you deserve."

"Let's see, why don't you wait until we go to New Orleans in December for your award presentation?" she said, and sighed. "Three days in paradise. Lord, I can't wait. I'm going to consume you."

"I think we'll consume each other. You're so sweet, Theda. You're everything I ever wanted in a woman…and more. Work on being free so we can be together."

A spasm of fear seized her then. Memory was

unforgiving. She remembered nights lying alone and wishing to die after Hunter had abandoned her. She remembered when Art and Kelly had died. *Was she such a coward?* Cowards never knew much happiness, she thought.

"I'm not the only one," she said softly. "*You* also have issues of trust, my darling. Even though after what Helena did to you, I don't blame you."

"Yeah," he agreed, thinking about how Helena had left him and Curt. He wondered if he could take it if Theda somehow proved untrue.

In the early-morning hours, Helena dreaded the morning sun. She looked at the drawn blinds and felt rage so deep she could hardly bear it. *So the bitch had won after all.* When Keatha and she had gotten home, they'd talked about the debacle for hours.

"Well, we knew they could prove the photo had been altered," Helena said. "We knew that from the start. We simply decided that it was worth the gamble."

How had she been such a fool? How could she have left Hunter for Carl? But she had and now she simply had to get Hunter back. Helena had the faith of demons in herself. When she wanted something, she saw nothing and nobody between that thing and herself. Well, she wanted Hunter and she damn well intended to have him again.

"It isn't over, Theda," she said vehemently, "not by a long shot."

Curt tossed, thinking about the meeting and wishing he could have gone. Had Dr. Coles won? Had she lost?

He couldn't see her losing. Folks were so crazy about her. Maybe if she lost, she'd move away and his mother and father could be together again. He didn't let himself think about Hunter following her. His mind was messing up these days. His dad was adamant about having a life with Theda and he didn't want to antagonize him too much. He missed the old closeness he'd had with Hunter and wanted it back.

But lying there Curt thought most of all he wanted some peace inside himself. His hormones were raging and he wished he could have gained solace from talking to Hunter about things. But how could he talk to his father when he was so mad with him for the way he was giving his mother the cold shoulder?

Chapter 16

Attorney Branch Haley had offices in D.C., Crystal Lake, which was his hometown, and Baltimore. He specialized in divorce cases and was considered one of the best divorce lawyers on the East Coast. He was renowned for his human touch, as well as his razor-sharp mind. He was a small, wiry man.

He and Hunter Davis sat in his office, drinking Turkish coffee and eating scones, as Hunter filled him in about the altered photos and Helena's attempts to discredit Theda. Branch was impressed with Hunter's credentials.

"What is it you'd like done?" Branch asked.

"I'm not sure." Hunter frowned. "I want Helena stopped. I'm wondering if her mind is going...."

"Has she ever shown signs of losing touch with reality?"

Hunter thought a long moment. "Once or twice she was hysterical around me."

The lawyer nodded. "I may need to know more about this."

Hunter drew a deep breath. Helena's hysteria had occurred on a lonely country road in Louisiana. He sincerely hoped it wouldn't be necessary to talk about it now.

With sensibilities honed from years of practice, Branch saw that this was a sore point for Hunter. "From what you tell me, there's a lot of jealousy going on here," the lawyer said.

Hunter nodded. "I also have a seventeen-year-old son who worships his mother. He's very protective of her. I don't want him hurt."

"Which makes our work harder. I need to mull this over," Branch said.

"What I want most of all is to stop her from ever hurting Theda again."

"Are you afraid she'll hurt her physically? Is your ex capable of violence in your estimation?"

Hunter pondered the question. "She has sprung at me in fits of anger. But, no, I can't say I'd consider her violent."

"You're sure, because it's important," Branch said. When Hunter didn't respond he continued. "It sounds to me like Helena still loves you—or believes she does," he said.

"The woman left me for another man." Hunter snorted. "Where was that love then?"

"She perhaps reconsidered after finding the grass wasn't greener." He smiled narrowly. "You're a catch, Mr. Davis. A big fish, if you will. This man possibly did things to her to cause her to appreciate you more."

Yes, Hunter thought bitterly, *he left her because she couldn't give him a child and that's my fault.* He couldn't speak of that now.

Branch Haley looked at him with compassion. "I'd like you to write to Helena, a carefully worded letter that would warn her against further acts of terror against Dr. Coles or you. I believe from what you've told me, she'll do little or nothing to hurt *you.* If she continues to sully Dr. Coles's reputation, a legal suit is a possibility. Your case, however, would be hard to prove.

"But first, I'd wait a bit, see what she does next.

Watch her. Tell her you've seen me. Let her know in no uncertain terms that you'll fight her. The worst mistake you could make would be to do nothing."

Hunter talked briefly with Theda in his car on his cell phone on the way home. He was very pleased at how well she'd weathered this whole situation. She was in her office with a student and couldn't talk, but he told her briefly about the visit to the lawyer. He hesitated when he said he was on his way to visit Helena and wondered why he hesitated. It surely wasn't something he looked forward to.

Finishing, she chuckled and said, "Well, you know, I-L-Y."

He laughed. That was their code for *I love you* if someone else was around.

At Hunter's home as he drove up, Helena waved at him from the porch stoop of Keatha's house. He had intended to go into his house for a few minutes, then go over to Keatha's. Now Helena stood up as he parked in the driveway and came over.

"Hunter?"

"Yes."

"How are you?"

"Why do you ask? Are you still trying to make trouble?"

"It's cold out here." She was warmly dressed. "Please don't make me leave. I want to talk with you."

He invited her into the house and the living room. They sat down.

Without preliminaries she began, "I know now how you felt when I left you. I'll never get over being sorry for that."

Her voice was softly seductive and it did nothing but irritate him. "You don't have to be sorry. I got over it long ago. I'm not going to beat about the bush, Helena. I'm talking with a lawyer. If you ever try to hurt Theda again, you'll have me to reckon with."

She recoiled from his bluntness. "You don't believe *I* sent that photograph?"

"I know you were right in there with Keatha."

"You're *wrong*," she said slowly, thinking Keatha was right. He could prove nothing. But it galled her to hear him defend Theda.

She plunged on. "We had something once, you and I. We could have that again. You've still got feelings for me. I know that."

"Then you know more than I do," he scoffed. He clenched his fists, then opened one hand and hit one fist into the open hand. "Come to your senses, Helena. It's *over* between us. It was over a long time ago. I want you to understand that Theda and I are in love and I won't let you hurt her. Not ever. Don't try any more stunts, and I think you'd better go now."

To his surprise, she rose and left without a backward glance. At the door she paused and turned around. Her face blazed with fury that shocked him. Anger thickened her voice as she told him, "I *won't* give you up, Hunter! I *can't* give you up!"

Chapter 17

"A winter wonderland!" many partygoers exclaimed as they came into the Crystal Lake city hall's huge gymnasium.

Theda, Hunter, Andre, Angela and her husband, Ken, were all early. Now Andre looked around him, smiling. "This is your baby," he told Theda, "and you can play the proud parent." Then to Angela, "As decorations chairperson, you really strutted your stuff."

This was the first year that the Harney High Faculty Dance was open to the entire community and the community was loving it. The gym was aglow with tiny, soft white lights, balloons, potted varicolored poinsettias, pinecones and chrysanthemums of every hue. The floors were polished to a high luster and the perfume of roses and gardenias was in the air.

Women were in their best, some in lush evening gowns and some in party dresses. Every single adult person had been invited and most had accepted. Hunter had brought his cameras and a young man home from college for Christmas had agreed to help him.

"The way you look tonight," Hunter told Theda, "I don't want to leave your side for a minute, but you'll want this recorded."

She playfully swatted him. In ivory silk and wool, off the shoulder, with long sleeves that ended in a point over her hands, her gown had been fashioned by Roland, D.C.'s premiere dress designer. Her ivory teardrop pearl earrings lent a glow. And if she had to say so herself, Theda had decided she looked really well. Her photo was the first one that Hunter snapped.

"Here's my battle plan for tonight," he said. "I take the photos at first for an hour or so, and I'll know I have the best of the lot. Then I devote my time mostly to you, leaving the rest to Fritz." This was the young man who helped him, a gangly brown youth with dimples and a shy smile.

Nick Redmond's combo played on the bandstand covered with red carpeting. The music was soft and quite magical. Theda and Angela had gotten their heads together. No way could they have afforded the fabulous Nick who was riding the crest of the entertainment waves, but Theda had known Nick when he was trying to get the ten-years-older Janet to marry him. He'd told her she had been very, very helpful and that he was forever in her debt. He had accepted her invitation, jumped at it, in fact.

"At last a chance to partly pay my debt to you," he'd said, laughing. And he was here with people already around the bandstand, ogling him and his group. Nick played piano, drums, saxophone, but his guitar was what said it all. People swore they got high just listening to Nick Redmond's thrilling guitar.

As Theda talked with Nick, Janet came up. "We don't see you enough," she said, hugging Theda and gleefully pulling out photos of her little girl.

Theda felt tears come to her eyes as she looked

at the photo of Nick, Janet and the child. It made her think of Art and Kelly. She waved to Hunter and beckoned him, and he came over, posing and taking pictures of the combo and Nick as he came.

Janet shrieked when Theda introduced Hunter. "Not *the* Hunter Davis? It has been too long."

"One and the same," Theda said proudly. "We really do have to get together."

"Tell me more and anytime," Janet answered.

The set was almost finished and Janet called to Nick to meet Hunter. The two men liked each other immediately.

"I've got a song request," Theda told Nick.

"Name it."

"'All I Want From You.'"

"You've got it and you'll hear it more than once."

"Thank you."

Nick went back to his group as Janet moved away with someone who wanted to dance.

Hunter looked at her with a grin. "Special song you're requesting. Old love?"

"Don't be nosy," she twitted him. "As a matter of fact, I'm requesting it for us because, sweetheart, all I want from you is everything. You'll love it. I promise."

"You look happy and that makes me happy. I'll be at your side for the rest of the time after the photos."

"Everybody's going to want a copy of the booklet you're planning to make of this party."

"I've thought about that and I'm going to give away copies—free. That should go over big."

"Oh, honey, that's wonderful! I'm glad you thought of that."

Looking at her shining face, he reflected that she had been through so much lately and it didn't show at all. He had been afraid of a huge fallout, that many people were going to punish her somehow, but that hadn't happened. There certainly had been gossip and after the night of the school board-community meeting, they had cooled it big. He had left her house earlier, but they still saw each other frequently. They were still as much in love as ever.

Theda did wonder, however, if the Crystal Lake men didn't look at her with more lustful eyes. It was more apparent tonight than it had been since the photos were mailed. But maybe it was just the splendor of the dress and her happiness that the Christmas Ball was beautiful beyond what she'd expected it to be.

Frank and Caroline Steele came up to her. Proud leaders of the once-popular group, The Singing Steeles, they had been two of her staunchest supporters, along with their three grown children. Annice Jones, a psychologist, had been a godsend when Kelly and Art had died. Theda still thought she'd go to consult with her about the retouched nude photos, but with Hunter's help, she was pulling through that. She introduced them to Hunter who said he'd want a photo a little later.

"Oh, Lord," Caroline said. "This party is the cat's pajamas and it's gorgeous. But it pales beside you and that dress. Roland?"

"Yes, and he'd be here if he wasn't in Europe."

"You don't have to tell me. Let me bring you up to date on my brood. Annice is in bed with flu and sends her love, Ashley is in Canada performing this week and Whit is in South America. Both send their love and good wishes." She looked suddenly sober as she took Theda's hand. "We talked, I know, and I would have been over, but Annice's flu was particularly nasty and I had to take care of her." She turned to Hunter. "I'm glad you were there to see after Theda. In fact, I'm glad about you, period. You're just what the doctor ordered."

"She's my heart," Hunter said. "I can never do enough for her."

"She's our heart, too," Frank said. "Hurt her and we'll go for you. I guess some people in this community found that out."

Two more couples came up in time to hear the end of that conversation and all four chimed in. Lance and Fairen Carrington looked happily in love, arm in arm. They had weathered their share of heartbreak when Lance had been accused of killing his then wife, Fairen's twin sister. Fairen was editor of the *Crystal Lake Eagle,* the city's thriving, award-winning newspaper. Her editorials on the nude-photo scandal had done so much to sway community support to Theda. Now they hugged, then hugged again.

"I've said it before," Theda told Fairen, "but I will never be able to repay you. You've made my life so much different than it would have been."

"Girl, you're our pride and joy," Fairen told her. "Our very own Ph.D. and generally wonderful woman. There's nothing we wouldn't do for you."

"Include us in that," a velvety voice chimed in and Maura and Josh Pyne hugged Theda, too. Two more of the town's pillars, Maura was an architect and Josh a builder. Maura had designed city hall; Josh had built it. Like others, Josh and Maura had rallied around Theda and Hunter. They had met Hunter and now Maura embraced him, too. The men shook hands.

Looking around, Maura's eyes narrowed as she looked at Theda with a playful grin. "You really have it all sewed up tonight. Wonderful gown, wonderful man, wonderful ball." Her voice went solemn. "You deserve it all, sweetie, and we're damned sure going to do whatever we can do to see that you get it."

Andre took the stage to welcome the revelers and Reverend Whisonant followed him. "Are we a great community or are we a great community?" Andre asked, and the crowd roared affirmation.

"We are a community of *love,*" Reverend Whisonant told them. "Not hate, not despair, not malice. We are a varied group, some rich, some poor, some well-educated, some who never got the chance. But we've proved ourselves to be a cohesive group who do amazing things and accomplish amazing goals.

"I pray that this will be the first of many get-togethers like this and that we will stay the people we are, a city under God and the Heavens, forgiving, caring, loving. *Forever!*"

So many people had backed her, Theda reflected now. Outpourings of love had come from the community and only a small amount of hostility. True, that small amount was headed by Keatha Ames and was virulent, but the love had crushed the hate. As Reverend Whisonant spoke of it being a community of love, Theda's eyes were drawn to the door and the ticket takers as Keatha and Helena walked in. The microphones were well amplified, so the two women had to hear Reverend Whisonant's words, but they didn't look toward the stage. They continued to the right and the cloakroom to check their coats.

Theda was determined not to let their presence remotely affect her night, but Hunter had told her what Helena had said to him about not letting him go and it bothered her. After thinking it over carefully, it didn't seem to her that Helena was losing it. The woman was just evil, she thought. Just thinking of Helena caused a chill to course through her, but she never had and never would let fear rule her life.

Theda found herself nearly fainting with delight at Hunter. In his black Italian broadcloth suit and scarlet tie, he attracted a lot of women's attention. His coal-black hair and obsidian eyes in his craggy face turned her on sky-high.

And Hunter's rangy, tall, fit body was driving her crazy. She sighed, wanting to be somewhere alone with him.

Just then Hunter took Theda in his arms to a lively waltz. As they swayed rhythmically, she told him, "Things surely have changed."

"Yeah, they sure have."

"Um-m-m." Suddenly a smile spread across her face and she pressed her cheek to his.

"You're looking bashful. Why?"

"I'm remembering the night of the school board–community meeting when we were waiting for voting results."

He threw back his head and laughed, then half closed his eyes as he held her away and looked at her. "You turn me on, baby, higher than the Alps. Theda. *Theda.*" He shook her slightly.

"And you turn me on," she said.

"We've got it for each other. We're always going to be together and in love. With us, old age is just going to be a number."

Both became aware of a vivid stir in the room and looked around to see Helena coming onto the dance floor in a scarlet chiffon gown, intricately draped and formfitting, with a nearly backless cut. She sparkled with rhinestones. Before she got a few steps onto the floor, someone had asked her to dance. She shook her head and came toward Theda and Hunter as the set ended.

"Hello, my darling," she said to Hunter. He looked at her sternly and nodded.

"And I guess hello is in order to you, too." Her gaze at Theda was glacial. Helena seemed high on some unknown substance, or perhaps on sheer female power.

Helena was not to be deterred. "I'm here as Keatha's guest. I don't think I got an invitation. Well, you're looking at me, Hunter. I chose this gown because you like backless ball gowns and my gown matches your tie. Will you dance with me?"

Hunter thought he didn't intend to be waylaid tonight by Helena. "Sorry," he said. "I'm afraid my dances are all taken."

Helena raised her eyebrows. "Too bad because I'm sure you'd like to hear the news I have for you. Peace may actually be in your future with me gone."

Both Hunter and Theda perked up. Helena carried a red lace and chiffon fan and she touched Hunter's face with it flirtatiously. "You're interested, I see." She turned cool eyes onto Theda. "Let him dance with me and you'll both be happy."

"In that case, by all means," Theda said evenly.

As Hunter reluctantly danced off, Andre, who had watched the whole tableau, walked up and held out his hand to Theda. They began the slow dance that gave them a chance to talk.

Andre held her close. "I'm not a man given to verbal superlatives," he told her, "but you are fabulous tonight. Are you getting over the bad scene? You seem to be, and God knows the community is supporting you."

Of course, she didn't tell him her feelings about certain men and their underhanded looks. She wondered wistfully if his high opinion of her had been lowered in any way. He was too smart for that, she thought. And she hadn't detected any change in his manner since the photos.

"Chairpersons of the various committees outdid themselves," Andre said. "This is a glorious affair. You can be proud that this was your idea."

"It is nice." She had been so wrapped up in Hunter that she had not truly appreciated the beauty of the hall. Now she looked around and was very satisfied. Then her eyes fell on Hunter and Helena as Helena pressed herself ever closer to Hunter. He looked uncomfortable.

Theda realized that she was more jealous of Helena than usual. Tonight Helena was a star. With her long black-silk hair and pale skin, her slender model's body that still had all the right curves, she was a vision and many male eyes were glued to her. She certainly had a strikingly hellish beauty.

Theda also saw Keatha on the sideline in stark black silk and emeralds. She seemed to monitor the room.

Mrs. Sanders, Kitty's mother, came to them as the set ended. Dressed in a short pale gray silk crepe dress, she was lovely and looked her age of early thirties rather than older as she did in her nurse's uniform. "You're going to love the food," she announced to them. "I checked about for favorite foods and I think nearly everybody has something special coming. We've got lots of Mexican food, too, German potato salad, as well as good old American potato salad. The New England clam chowder is about the best I've tasted." She smiled broadly. "The caterers are setting up now and I have to go supervise."

Out of the corner of her eye, Theda saw Hunter snapping photos again, and reflected that he hadn't come back to her after his dance with Helena.

Andre smiled at her. "I'm just going to check out everything," Andre said. "Save me a few dances."

"Of course."

Hunter came back to her as Andre walked away. She couldn't help teasing him. "I thought I'd lost you," she said.

"Never happen." He grinned. Was she going to have to ask him? "Did you enjoy your dance with Helena?" Did she sound waspish? she wondered.

"What's to enjoy? Same old Helena. All games and little or no honesty."

"Did she say anything of interest?"

"Just that there's something Keatha has to make a phone call about tonight while she's here. Then, she tells me we'll both to happy to hear the news."

"I'll believe it when I hear it, and even then—"

He held out his arms and she moved into them as the band played "All I Want From You."

"Hey, I like this," Hunter declared, pulling her

closer, inhaling her perfume and her natural fragrance.

"Any tighter," she teased him, "and I'm going to just melt into you."

"I wish," Hunter said.

He squeezed her hard and quickly.

That set was longer than most because the revelers demanded a couple of encores. Theda found that she was happy beyond what she had expected to be. Without Helena, the night would have been perfect. *With* Helena, you never knew what would happen next and it dampened her joy to know that this woman intended to cause her grief as long as she could.

Chapter 18

As the evening progressed the combo began to play salsa music. Everybody wanted to dance to the lively music. Hunter was superb at the dance, but Theda wasn't far behind. Even Reverend and Mrs. Whisonant shook their booties with grace.

But it was when Helena took the floor and began to dance that people stood still and took notice. She was spectacular. Her scarlet chiffon was a flame as it flashed. Murmurs of admiration rose around her.

Theda slowed her steps. "I think she's trying to get your attention," she told Hunter.

He looked at his ex-wife and began to frown. "She's Curt's mother and I don't want the whole place talking about how she performed here," he said.

She couldn't help saying it. "The way *I'm* being talked about."

That was an unfair assessment and he pointed it out. "You were a victim of mischief. This is willful."

But somehow she wondered if he were not concerned beyond Curt. She saw tonight how exciting the woman could be and it bothered her. They must have known passion together, Hunter and Helena. They must have lain in each other's arms and made explosive love. She felt a jealous knife through her heart and she shuddered. She was going to have to do better than this.

Willing herself to calmness, she concentrated on the salsa and let her body move to the rhythm, the beat of the drums. The room throbbed with the beat.

Drunk on her own power, Helena swayed her hips toward Hunter and held out her hands. Her voice was throaty as she told him, "Remember how we used to dance the salsa, then go home and make the most exciting love?"

"Helena, stop it!"

But there was no stopping Helena now. She flung her arms around Hunter and kissed him hard on the mouth. He quickly disengaged her arms and pushed her away. "Stop this nonsense, *now!*" He spoke to her as he would have to a recalcitrant child.

Helena swallowed hard. "Sorry. I can no more stop loving you than I can stop my heart from beating!"

A hush had begun to fall over the space surrounding them.

Hunter turned to Theda and hugged her tightly and she could hear his heart drumming beats of love. He put his mouth to her ear and tongued it, then whispered. "Please, sweetheart, pay her no mind. She means to hurt you and I won't let her, I promise you."

Reverend Whisonant drew Helena aside. "You have a son to consider," he said acidly. "Madam, I beg that you consider him."

His dart might have struck home, but Helena had tunnel vision. "All's fair in love and war," she murmured, "and I *mean* to have Hunter back."

Reverend Whisonant felt helpless against her one-track mind, but his money was on Theda. He knew love when he saw it.

Later, a huge old-fashioned jukebox played golden oldies tunes as the revelers ate.

Mrs. Sanders stood as proud as a peacock near the groaning tables. Roast beef, chicken, spiral hams and turkey all were golden brown. There was delicious New England clam chowder. Carved raw vegetables, candied yams, macaroni and cheese graced the long tables. A special table of desserts of luscious cakes, pies and ice cream for those hardy enough to eat it stood in an alcove. And there was the beverage table with hot mulled cider, hot chocolate, coffee and tea.

Theda and Hunter set their plates on a nearby table and snagged two flutes of champagne from a passing waiter.

Raising his glass, he waited for her to raise hers. The crystal rang. "To us," he said simply, "forever."

She looked at him with her heart in her eyes. If she lost him again, could she take it? But she felt herself to be a strong woman who had weathered many of fate's blows. One thing she knew, she'd fight for their love.

Helena stood demurely at a distance surrounded by men, a couple of whose wives came and got them.

"She's certainly holding court," Theda said.

"That's her style."

Theda liked the fact that Hunter didn't talk meanly about women and his mildly sarcastic comments about Helena were as far as he'd go. He had been like this long ago. She had liked it then; she liked it now. But then he was a man who loved women and she was glad to be his special woman.

"Can you leave early?" he asked.

"Yes. Angela will take over and Andre won't mind."

She went to the spacious dressing room then and found Angela there. Her friend put a hand on each of her shoulders. "The more I see of Helena Reid the less I like her and there wasn't much room to travel in the beginning."

"She's quite a character."

"The woman's shameless."

"We're leaving early. Will you take over for me?" Theda asked.

"You know I will," Angela replied.

"Now, go home and make the wildest love

you're capable of for a long time and wake up in paradise."

Theda grinned. "Mother's recipes for happiness."

When dancing resumed, Theda and Hunter were together near the edge of the floor. It was a slow piece and Helena came for Hunter again. This time he flatly turned her down, but she wouldn't be denied. "I have the answer you both want to hear," she said throatily. "The kiss was for old time's sake and I won't apologize. Dance with me and you won't be sorry. I promise."

Hunter looked at Theda who nodded. "Go ahead."

They moved away and she saw Andre come toward her and smiled softly at him. He held out his arms and she went into them.

In the car on the way to Theda's house, Hunter drove to the waterfront and parked. A lone guard stood a distance away. There was a half moon waning and the water was choppy, blue-green in the moonlight.

"You're awfully quiet," he told her.

"I guess I am. Just thinking. I'm happy that

we'll be going to New Orleans for your award a few days after the holiday."

"Yeah, so am I. I've got some plans for you that will tingle your toes for the rest of your life when you think back about it."

"Oh, now, have you?"

"Yeah, we're staying at a lush hotel in the French Quarter, with balconies surrounded by hedges. The weather is not too cold and we can wrap up and make love on the balcony. It will be a dream you won't want to wake up from."

She could only wonder if Helena would be out of their lives by then. He hadn't said what Helena had told him the last time they danced. Now she asked him, and he said, "She told me things are looking up and she's planning to go back to Texarkana…."

"Why didn't you tell me right away?"

"I wanted you to ask me," he teased her, "and yeah, I'm not sure she's on the level. Helena is such a liar. I'm sure you're upset about the way she showed off tonight."

"It did cross my mind. Are you ever going to be able to stop her?"

"I'm doing my best. She knows she's lost. That's why she's behaving so badly."

"Does she? You two have a deep history."

"Not like *our* history, yours and mine." He leaned forward and kissed her throat, unbuttoning her coat. Then he thought of her dancing with Andre and he said without meaning to, "I'm sure Andre has no crazy woman in *his* past."

"That's unfair. Andre is a very nice man. He helped me through a very painful time."

"I know, and I'm grateful. He *is* a nice guy. Do you wish I hadn't come? Especially now?"

She hesitated a fraction too long and it hurt him. He had cost her and he knew it. Not if, but how much regret did she have? He shouldn't have asked it, but he couldn't help himself. He had watched her dance almost cheek to cheek with Andre Lord and daggers of jealousy had sliced through him. "How close were you and Lord before I came back to you?"

She didn't hesitate. "You want to know if I slept with him."

"Did you?"

"Would it matter if I did?"

He crushed her to him. "Hell no, it wouldn't matter. Because I've got you now and believe me, baby, I'm not letting go."

Her voice was cool even as she thrilled to his

hot mouth on her throat and face, at the corners of her mouth and finally when his mouth ravaged hers in a searing kiss. She drew away from him dizzy with love and confusion.

"I'm not sure it's entirely up to you."

Breathing deeply, he started the car and with the motor purring, said, "It's up to *me*. Let's go home and make love all night."

"You're supposed to be protecting me from gossip, remember?"

She was only half joking. She found she didn't like the idea of Andre listening to gossip about Hunter spending whole nights at her house. Her body asserted itself and she wanted Hunter's arms around her, wanted his throbbing length inside her walls and his mouth on her tender breasts. But she wanted security, too, a life without Helena and her hellish taunts and actions. She had a choice and she wondered for a only few seconds what it should be.

Chapter 19

New Orleans was one of the world's most fascinating cities, even with the devastation it had suffered, Theda and Hunter thought. Many of the people had come back, as charming, as friendly as ever. Now in a rented car on Elysian Fields and headed toward Gentilly Boulevard, Theda placed her hand on Hunter's knee.

"It brings back memories," she said softly. "We were so young then."

"Yeah, although I've been back many times. I guess you're always attracted to the place where you were born, even if your parents and relatives moved away."

"You haven't mentioned if you still have friends here."

"I had. They were flooded out and chose not to return."

In the next two hours they covered a lot of territory.

They spent time in the destroyed Ninth Ward that had been largely leveled. Sadness rose in both their breasts as they talked about how this hadn't had to happen. They were both very somber when they moved on to another part of the city.

Now they neared the famous Catholic edifice, St. Louis Cathedral. Standing outside, admiring the little-damaged place, they parked and got out, stood in awe as people went in and out. "It's so beautiful," Theda said. "You feel the presence of God here. Are we going in?"

"Not today because I want to spend some time inside before we leave. The priest who was here before the hurricane wanted me to do extensive photos. I didn't have time then. Now I wish I had done before *and* after shots. I did a lot of photos just after the hurricane and it broke my heart.

Honey, you just can't imagine the devastation, the misery. It's a study in human frailty. I'll be coming back this spring or summer with you with me."

"In summer please, so we can stay awhile."

"Great. I want to talk to the priest before we leave this time."

After visiting the art museum, the Cabildo, with its timeless, shabby charm, they went back to the Ninth Ward and tears filled both their eyes. Theda had been so happy to read that an influential collegiate group had finished studies that showed this ward could be rebuilt with much less money and effort than had once been thought necessary. This meant the work could get underway sooner than expected.

"A study in human blundering," Hunter said, "and a damned shame. I hope it never happens again."

They made a brief tour of the famed French Quarter with its streets that were little crowded in the afternoon. At night, people would be out like ants seeking the hot music and the even hotter other entertainment. They would be at the awards ceremony, so they had decided to make the round of the Quarter the next night, then leave at noon two days later.

They were in front of Dooky Chase's, the wonderful restaurant run by a Creole couple whose parents had credentials dating back nearly a hundred years. A family-owned-and-run establishment, it was noted for its warmth and its excellent Creole food. Hunter's cell phone trilled and she listened. It had not rung since they arrived.

"Curt! Wassup?" Hunter smiled as he listened to his son, who sounded a bit nervous.

"Hey, Dad, how's it going?"

"I asked first."

"I mean, how's New Orleans?"

"And I repeat, I asked first. Is everything okay with you?"

"Yeah, I guess. Mom's a mess. She's moping around and she's upset about something, but she won't tell me what it is."

Hunter thought he knew what it might be. A letter could have reached her from his lawyer. "Your mom's a big girl. She can handle whatever. Just concentrate on your life, Curt. You're sure that's all?"

"Yeah, that's enough. Dad, it makes me sad that you two aren't getting closer."

"There's a lot of sadness in the world, Curt. We have to get used to it."

The boy was adamant. "I'm going to keep hoping anyway."

"You're sure that's all you need to tell me?"

"Yeah. I miss you more than I thought I would." He hesitated a few moments before he said, "We're not as close as we used to be. I wish we still were."

"I still feel close to you, son. I always will. I'm on your side forever."

"Thanks, Dad." Curt's voice brightened. "I'm staying with Mrs. Smith the way you wanted me to. Mom was mad, though. She wanted me to stay with them, but—Mrs. Ames just isn't my cup of tea. She's going away for a couple of days tomorrow and Mom said she'd be alone and lonely."

"Your mother will be just fine."

"Uh-huh. Well, tell Dr. Coles I said hello."

"I will." He didn't ask if Curt wanted to talk with Theda because he didn't think he would. It was enough for right now that he'd thawed enough to tell her hello.

Cutting off, Hunter looked at Theda as he put the phone back in his shirt pocket.

"Curt's not a happy camper," he said slowly.

"Something's really bothering him." They had talked about the lawyer writing Helena a letter. "I wonder if she's gotten the letter yet."

"Could be," Theda said.

The St. Charles Hotel is one of the most beautiful in the Crescent City and one of the smaller dining rooms where the awards dinner was held fit right in with that beauty. All award recipients had been asked to be early and they were. Theda wore a short jade silk jersey. She looked at Hunter in his black silk and wool gabardine suit, his black silk tie and snow-white linen and smiled. He was getting glances from beautifully dressed women in the room. *Back off, ladies, the gentleman goes home with me!*

The awards ceremony began early and many awards were given. The Photographic Society of America was one of the most prestigious in the country and the platinum statues they gave were much coveted by photographers. He introduced her to many friends, their wives and their girlfriends. She was surprised at the number of women photographers there with their husbands and friends.

At the brief cocktail hour, they milled about,

talked about their work. Hunter's book on South Africa was prominently displayed and sales were brisk. He signed books for a long while with his bold flourish.

Theda met congressmen, dignitaries, diplomats. This was quite an affair, she thought. Then finally after others had received their awards, Hunter received his. He got a rousing ovation for his work and his book.

Theda felt so proud of him, she thought her heart would burst when he began his speech. "Ladies and gentlemen, I am as honored as a man can be and I thank you for the opportunity to be here tonight."

Hunter talked mostly of hope and perseverance, and it was of New Orleans that he talked most. Those in his audience were rapt listeners. He did not talk long, reminding them that "Tonight we are in a dazzling city with much to see. We have a banquet to savor, dancing for some of us." He grinned then. "The French Quarter awaits our forays into it to listen to music heralded around the world."

The audience laughed heartily. Hunter ended with, "I thank you from the bottom of my heart for this award, for your support and for your priceless fellowship."

The applause was deafening. The camaraderie in the room was palpable. Hunter was swamped as he moved from the podium.

Dinner was a lavish affair with china, crystal and gleaming silverware. The crystal chandelier was breathtaking. It was one of the best dinners Theda had ever eaten with succulent, crisply browned roast quail as their choice, artichoke hearts, baby corn and tiny green peas and onions. They wanted no dessert and settled for the thick Turkish coffee and one small piece of decadent dark chocolate candy.

Dancing on the domed roof was lovely, she thought, but somehow she couldn't get past the sadness that was now the city, in spite of its forced gaiety. But, no, she thought, it wasn't forced. The people of New Orleans were a gay people and little got them down. They knew very well that they would be back as happy as ever in a very little while.

Theda congratulated him. "You were spectacular." She laughed then. "You *are* spectacular."

"Thank you, but I believe you have that honor."

In their hotel room they had champagne on ice sent up and listened to jazz records. "Jazz goes to the heart," he said slowly. "It talks to what in us feels deeply about life and love." The champagne sat in its bucket, waiting.

In the bedroom they undressed. He put on cotton pajamas and a jacquard robe. She wore a sheer, lace nightgown and flowing peignoir. The color of the nightwear complimented Theda's cinnamon-colored, silken skin. Hunter looked at her with his eyes half closed.

"So the night begins," he said softly.

"Honey, I've got news for you. The night began long ago."

"It begins here for me."

"You can say that after that important award?"

"You're more important to me."

"You don't mean that."

"Don't I?"

She sat on his knee on the king-sized bed. "We need a twin bed for tonight."

"Yeah. Or no bed at all. This carpet makes a nice love pallet."

"Could we put on our coats and go out on the balcony?"

"You want to?"

"I do. I hate ever missing a full moon."

"You want it. You've got it."

She thought they were as close as two people could be. His muscular body was so beautiful. He went to the closet to get light coats and she lay back on the bed with her eyes closed. His cell phone rang and he called from the living room, "Honey, please get that."

Turning on Talk she said hello and the voice from hell came through asking to speak with Hunter.

Of course she recognized her, but asked anyway. 'May I say who's calling?"

"You know damned well who's calling. It's Helena. Put Hunter on."

Hunter came into the room and she handed him the phone, watching the deep frown on his face a second later. Helena's voice was loud, but she couldn't hear what was being said. She got up and went into the living room.

Hunter stood near the door, angry and frustrated. The last thing he wanted was to talk with Helena.

Chapter 20

Helena couldn't remember a time when she'd felt more frustrated. As she talked with Hunter, she thought about Keatha's being away, about Hunter's having insisted that Curt stay with Angela Smith. She hated being alone.

"I got a letter from your lawyer today," she told Hunter.

"And?"

"The letter warned me not to cause further trouble to your mistress—"

Hunter was furious. "Cut the crap, Helena. I

have no wife and when I do, it'll be Theda, so she isn't my mistress."

"I keep forgetting," Helena lied. Then, "Hunter, don't do this to me. I didn't send those photos and I don't know who did, but I won't have you threatening me because of Theda Coles. Yes, I hate her and I admit it. What do you plan to do? Have me put in prison for what you imagine I did?"

"Helena, please talk sense."

"You should be thinking about protecting me. I'm your son's mother."

"A fact I'm not always proud of."

Helena was crying then. "I hurt you, I know, but I had another husband and thanks to you, he put me out. My life is ruined, Hunter, and you ruined it. You owe me big-time, and I will never let you forget it. Okay, try protecting your damned woman, if you can."

Helena hung up then and Hunter went out to the living room where Theda sat on the sofa. He stood for a long moment looking down at the nimbus of her reddish brown hair in the soft lamplight. He saw how upset she was and he sat down and put his arms around her. She drew away.

"We have to talk," she said, her voice hoarse with emotion. "I don't want my life to go on like this."

Hunter felt sick in the pit of his belly and he was angry.

"I love you, Hunter, the way I know I'll never love again, but I'm not going to be at the mercy of a madwoman. I'm going back in the morning." She had not known she would say it.

Panic flooded him as he saw the torment on her face and again he tried to take her in his arms. Again she pulled away. The time had come to tell her what had haunted him for so long. Then she'd know what a beast he could be, but he couldn't stand losing her. He leaned forward and pulled her resisting body to him. He held her so tightly he could feel the drumming of her heart and he felt tears scald his eyes. "You need to know," he said. "You've always needed to know, but I've never talked about it except briefly to a therapist."

She relaxed a bit as he said, "Please listen and please don't judge me."

She shook her head. "I won't judge you."

He drew a deep breath. "Helena called tonight because she got a letter from my lawyer telling her not to continue harassing you. I meant to talk with you about it on the plane, but we had that turbulence and engine trouble and I didn't get to it. We've been on the run since we got here. A postal inspector found a woman in a post-office branch in Baltimore who remembers part of the special delivery mailing and she remembers the woman who mailed them. She pretty much identified a photo of Helena, but she refuses to testify. That's all the evidence we have and that's all they were able to dredge up. Helena called because she got the letter and she's furious. She knows I mean business and I mean to protect you."

"And you also mean to protect her," Theda said.

"No. We can get a restraining order if she tries to harm you further. I don't think she'd ever physically attack you."

Quite bitterly Theda said, "With the way she operates, she wouldn't need to."

He wanted nothing so much as to make love to her, storm her defenses, make her his own again, but she was closed against him. His thoughts were swarming crazily and he knew then that he had to tell her the whole story. He cleared his throat and began.

"A little over three years ago, Helena visited a friend in Jackson, Mississippi and she asked me to come there. I did and she asked me to drive out on the Jackson to Vicksburg highway, a hilly area. Almost to Vicksburg I parked, and she told me that she was leaving me. She was marrying another man we both knew well, Carl Reid. She said she'd been seeing this man since I'd been traveling—a long time. She said that I'd left her alone too much and she was tired of it. I'd wanted her to travel with me, but she never would.

"She cut my heart out. I begged her to reconsider. No, I didn't love her the way I love you, but we had a family, a son. She laughed at me, said Reid was the man she'd wanted all her life and now she had him. He was older, richer, more powerful. Married and divorced three times. By then, her father was dead—he would have been on my side. I can't describe the despair I felt when she told me she'd slept with Reid since I left the first time. She said she was sure I slept around and I hadn't. She was covering her own betrayal. I was numb, but I said okay, go ahead, leave with your lover.

"She said then that she would sue for custody of Curt, that she could prove that my being away so much made me less fit than she was to have him."

He was silent then, remembering. It had been a nightmare then. It was still a nightmare. He should have dealt with this long ago, but he'd been running all this time. Now a sheer wall of harrowing memory stopped him cold and he shuddered.

"I knew that with Reid's money and his lawyers, there was a good chance she could make good on her threat and I lost it. I told you we were parked and she'd said, 'That's all. I'm ready to go back now.'"

"We had driven almost to Vicksburg and the roads are hilly. I didn't want her to see me cry, but I couldn't help it. I begged her again to reconsider, and she laughed at me, told me, 'Next time, when you have a treasure, you won't go running off to the ends of the world and leave it.'

"Then I got mad, said I'd fight to keep Curt and surely the fact that she was having an affair would take care of that. She laughed again and said who would know? She'd swear it wasn't true and so would he. She'd blindsided me and I couldn't think.

"'Let's go back,' she'd said again, and I started up. My enemy was destroying me, and I had to fight back." Memories crushed him then and he choked as he tried to go on. Theda drew him to her and pressed his head to her bosom. His hot tears wet her gown as she stroked his back.

"Sweetheart, stop a while if it hurts too much," she told him.

"No. I should have told you long ago." He sat up and continued. She put her hands on his, then stroked them.

"Helena was frightened. She begged me to slow down. I've always prided myself on my control of myself and this was the way she knew me. But she didn't know me any longer and I didn't know myself. I was blinded by tears when I passed an 18-wheeler going up a hill, met a car on top of that hill and crashed.

"The other driver was hurt, but he recovered. I had a broken leg, but Helena was badly hurt. She stayed in the hospital for three weeks and the doctors said her reproductive system was injured and she might have to have a hysterectomy. When they told us, she got hysterical and accused me of trying to kill her.

"Carl Reid came to the hospital and confronted me. She begged me not to tell him that she might have to have the hysterectomy and I agreed. She rallied quickly and went on a vacation to the Canary Islands, Tenerife, Spain. Puerto de la Cruz. She called me and said she'd had to have the hysterectomy there. 'I'm trying not to hate you,' she'd told me. 'You've ruined my life. I wanted children with Carl and he wanted them. I hope God can forgive you, because I sure as hell never will.'"

He was silent for long moments and Theda could only say, "You were badly hurt the way no one should ever be. Sweetheart, be kind to yourself and remember, God forgives even a mortal sin." She leaned forward and kissed his eyes that were wet with tears.

His voice sounded strangled as he asked her, "Can you understand now why I even felt relieved when she came to Crystal Lake and declared herself still in love with me? At first it meant she'd at least forgiven me for injuring her, then when I knew she'd had a hand in sending those altered photos I was afraid she was losing it and I've felt even guiltier at costing her her mind.

"Maybe you're right to leave me. You know I'd give my life to protect you, but I can't know where this leads. I can't ask you to continue with me if you feel you can't. Where do we go from here, my darling?" He looked so helpless and her heart was torn up for him.

The floodgates of passion opened for her then and everything in her yearned for him to be closer than close to her. She wanted him inside her, both possessing each other in a fever that swept and held them both in thrall. She pressed his head back to her bosom and held it there and he felt her heart drumming, drumming with a beat that soothed him and eased his torment. Love filled them both and both knew that they were forever bound and there could be no turning back.

She stood up and slid the straps from her shoulders, letting the gown fall and pool around her ankles. Looking at her lush soft curves, his shaft rose rock hard. He bent to extricate her feet from the fabric and rubbed her foot across his face, kissing the instep, tonguing it lightly.

Hell, he thought, go all the way, and a pedicured toe went into his mouth to be sucked on gently. He heard her moan and it lured him on as she bent above him.

After a long while, Hunter stood and held out his hand to her, clasped her hand. "I'll get the champagne," he told her, "then we'll go to the bedroom."

"What if I want to stay here?"

He smiled roguishly. "We're going to need the bedroom, love. It's soundproof." He kissed her, nuzzled her neck, then tongued the corners of her mouth.

In the bedroom she went to the closet and took out a large crystal bottle of liquid, opened it and brought it back, passing it under his nose.

"Smells good, like an orange," he said. "What is it?"

"Sweet essence of orange, the safe-to-ingest kind. You just rub it on and like magic, you go up in flames."

"We don't need it, you know."

"Try it, you'll like it."

He took the bottle and set it on the dresser, took her lush naked body in his arms and began to caress her. His mind was clearing fast. Talking with her had relieved him of so much guilt because she understood where he was coming from and empathized. And for the first time since they were young, he felt free to love her again as completely as he ever had, and more. He impatiently waited now for her to be free of her fears so they could marry.

"I need a massage and I need to massage you," she told him.

"Anything you want, you get."

She lay back on the chaise lounge and he took the oil and spread it thinly on her body as she directed. Then he massaged her, kneading the silken flesh, the heels of his hands digging in as she murmured tender things to him. She had taken training in massage and had taught him some of the steps. Setting the bottle back on the dresser, he simply stood and looked down at her, his brain fogged with wanting her. Then she got up. She was slow, tantalizing, getting the bottle and having him lie down while she massaged him.

"You're so beautiful," she said. He lay beneath her ministrations, his muscular body pulsing, his shaft swollen with wanting to be inside her. She took her time, kneading him as he had done to her, enjoying the feel of his smooth, leathery flesh, loving the way his muscles rippled under her touch. He got up and poured them flutes of champagne. Giving it to her, she jostled his arm when she took it and champagne spilled on her belly.

"That's an invitation if ever I saw one," he said, laughing, and he bent and licked the liquid off her. Then he poured a little more on her breasts and belly and licked that off.

He positioned her and began to kiss her all over, then he knew he'd finish too fast and he kissed her belly, tonguing the indention and tonguing down to the core of her as she bucked above him. On his knees, his tongue flashed fire in her core then and her bud felt the glory of its loving as he expertly laved her. She held his head hard in to her, gripping the short strands of hair, stroking his face. He held her buns and squeezed them gently, then harder and she screamed his name and felt the rush of passion as she began her orgasm.

He leaned against her, still hearing his name echo when she'd screamed it.

He got up grinning. "Like that?"

"What do you think?" she murmured.

"Well, the lady screamed my name like she loves me." He stood looking down at her. "The bed calls to us."

She helped him slip on a condom from the nightstand. The big water bed swayed under their weight and she quickly spread her legs and he entered her, big and throbbing, already swollen. Inside the honeyed, slick walls of her, he felt his full power and he played her like the master he was. She purposefully gripped him with her tight inner walls, then released him and he shuddered. "Baby, let me last. I'm having a hard time holding out."

But she wanted him to have release so she teased him with her body, writhing and grinding, making her inner walls clutch him tightly in mock orgasm. He smiled and shook her. "You're asking me to shortchange you. Is that what you want?"

"Um-m-m. I want you to feel the way you made me feel. Come on, lover, give me all you've got."

With a last writhe and grind, she gripped him and he exploded. She held him in to her and kissed his face with tiny, wet kisses. "Thank you," she whispered, "for the first and for the second loving."

He drew deep breaths and shuddered slightly. "That was so good."

He rolled off her and propped himself on an elbow. "I could have lasted longer. I just didn't want to come. I felt like I wanted to stay in you forever."

"And I wanted you to, but you deserve release, too, the way you gave it to me."

They got more champagne and sipped it, moving naked to the kitchenette where a crystal tray of huge strawberries and cherries dipped in chocolate awaited them. She popped one into his mouth and he took it, then her finger. "I swear, I don't know which is sweeter," he said.

"You're the sweet one," she responded. Then

for a moment she was sober remembering what they'd talked about tonight. It had drawn them closer and she knew as she never had the depths of her love, of *their* love. "Don't we need music?"

He shook his head. "No. You're all the music I need tonight. Later maybe. I'm just getting started and I'm raging." He glanced down at his penis that stood at half-mast and smiled. "The old boy is just resting. He means to really get it on."

They ate more strawberries and cherries, fine Swiss cheese and oyster crackers, then the small ham, turkey and roast beef sandwiches that had been prepared for them.

"I've got an idea," she said. "We were going to put on our coats and go out on the balcony."

"Okay, but I love being naked with you."

"Lots more chances."

They put on coats and went out. It was cool in the early morning, but not too cool. A full moon hung low and both admired it. "It's there just for us," she said. "A January lover's moon."

Surrounded by tall shrubs, hidden from others, he took a condom from the robe pocket, opened her coat and held her in to him, entered her and squeezed her buns as she gasped with pleasure. Her breasts against his chest were doing wild things to him as she rubbed her pebbled nipples against him.

"I could take you out here for hours," he said. "I don't think I'll ever get enough of you."

He took her face in his hands and savaged her mouth until his kisses hurt a little, but she pressed in to him, lips slightly swollen, hungry for much more. "Oh, my darling," she whispered, "what is there about you that makes you so good?"

"It's gotta be love, baby, the way I love you and you love me."

The cool air caressed their bodies bared under the coats and partly exposed as they went through the ancient mating dance and each reveled in the wonder of it all. A full moon and a galaxy of stars seemed to him no more beautiful than she was.

They were out on the balcony for a long while as they saved themselves for more and more. As they entered the apartment, she got a condom from the pocket of her robe. In the living room, she pushed him back on the big armless chair and straddled him. She teased him by sitting just above his lap and letting just the tip of his shaft touch her.

"You want me?" she teased him. "Show me how much you want me."

He took it as long as he could, then pulled her down hard as he entered her forcefully, going into the honeyed wetness that did not let it hurt. "Does that answer your question?"

She leaned against him, put her face close to his and whispered all the naughty things in his ear that turned him on. Then she licked his face and kissed his mouth from side to side as he groaned. "There ought to be a law against women like you driving men like me crazy."

She laughed. "There probably is such a law but I'm ignoring it. I own you, you told me, so I can do with you what I will."

"Does that go for both of us? Take care what you answer."

"It does. Lover, do with me what you will." Her face was merry, warm with lust and to him achingly lovely.

He took her at her word and worked her evenly and well, using every bit of experience and mastery he knew. Tears filled her eyes at the hotness of the passion and the thrills that flashed through her. He kept pressing her down and the power of him that came up to her soft body held a wonder of its own. She pressed her breasts onto his rock-hard chest and her mouth covered his with a hunger so intense she couldn't believe it. They came together and she moaned in the back of her throat and cried out. His groans came from the heart and soul of him. It was a special time for them, a coming together as never before. The beginning of a lifetime together and both knew it with joy in their hearts.

Chapter 21

Curt pulled up in his driveway and sighed as he looked first at his house, then at Keatha's. Where was his mother? Both houses were dark, and she never went to bed early. He drove into the garage and decided not to go in immediately. He went around the house and switched on the back yard floodlights, got his basketball from a storage space outside and began shooting hoops. Oh, yes, he chuckled, he got game.

He was doing all right, he thought, as his rangy form twisted and swiveled, bringing the ball back and forth, over his back, dribbling. He was no Michael Jordan, but he wished his dad could see him now. His mom didn't care much for sports. She wanted him to be a highly successful businessman like his former stepdad, but the business side of photography was all that interested him.

With half an ear he listened for the sound of Helena's car in the driveway as he played.

After a while he went in and turned on the lights in the living room. He thought about his dad and Dr. Coles in New Orleans. Together, they sure lit up a room, but his heart went out to his mother wanting his dad back the way she did. She had seemed a little better the last day or so, livelier, as if she looked forward to something, and that made him happy. He was really tired, but he didn't want to go to bed. The next day was Saturday and he could sleep late. He decided to go over to Mrs. Ames and wait for his mother. He wanted to sweet-talk her into lending him her car so his could go into the shop.

He let himself into Keatha's house with his key and settled down in the library alcove just off the living room. The alcove was filled with books, but missing books let you see some portions of the other room. The sofa there was deep and restful and he was very tired. It had been good talking with his dad. He got up and snapped off the light. He'd surprise his mother when she came in, spring out at her. She always enjoyed a good laugh.

Soon he fell into a deep sleep, but he woke what seemed about an hour later to the sound of low voices. He heard murmuring and low, hushed giggling and laughter. He became dimly aware of soft lights on. He alternately squeezed his eyes shut and opened them wide to focus and he breathed shallowly. He perked up then at murmured endearments and sexual entreaties. Riveted with horror, he realized it was his mom's voice begging for sex from a stranger who answered her in muffled, but unmistakable tones. A ragged sob rose in his throat.

Boiling with fury, he peeped through the opening in the books and saw them leaning against a table, the strange man's hand under her skirt, raising it high, and her legs around…

Sick with shock, he came out from behind the bookcase, yelling, "Mom, what the *hell* are you doing?"

She was either drunk or lost in ecstasy. For a minute, they clung together. Then Helena looked at Curt with wide, startled eyes and tried to push her lover away.

Curt came all the way into the room, glaring at the two. Then he raised his arm. *"Get out!"* He screamed at the man, his voice guttural, murderous. His fists were clenched tight and his nose and eyes wet and burning.

"Yeah, well," the stranger said evenly, "I was just leaving." He grinned a sickly grin as he turned, then turned back and said, "Now, don't hurt your mama, boy. We grown-ups lose our heads sometimes."

After the man left, Curt turned to his mother. If his glances had been bullets, Helena would have been dead. But she stood her ground.

"When you're older, you'll understand that grown-ups sometimes lose their heads." He wanted to laugh hysterically. She was repeating her lover's words.

"I've been so lonely," she pleaded in a soothing voice. "And your dad spends all his time with that whore."

Curt nearly lost it then, and he grated, "Don't call Dr. Coles what *you* are."

"I just want your dad and me…"

"Stop it! You want just what you were getting."

She started toward him. "Honey, please forgive me. It will never happen again." She had every confidence that she could sway him.

As she continued to come forward, putting out her hand to touch him, to change his mind, she murmured something he couldn't understand and he said, "Don't touch me! Stay away from me. I never want to see you again!"

Curt had presence enough of mind to realize he wasn't wholly functioning, but sleep had fled. He went into the house and let himself into the garage and his car. He had to get away from this place, away from Helena. He would never call her *Mom* again. Scalding tears ran down his face and he angrily tried to brush them away. His heart hurt so bad it scared him and his balled fists wanted to hit something, anything. He had to get away. He backed the car out of the garage and drove blindly into the night.

Chapter 22

Out on the highway, Curt thought about the fact that his brakes had been giving him a bit of trouble. Snow had been pushed back off the highway, but there were patches of ice and black ice and he'd have to be careful.

He glanced at the clock on the dashboard—1:25 a.m. Then, out of the corner of his eye, he glanced down the steep incline by the road. Lots of ice down there.

Later, he would wonder what happened.

The car skidded, went off the road and then was

rolling over and over down the steep, icy incline until it came to rest, caught on a big tree branch halfway to the bottom. Then it was pitch-black.

At ten o'clock that same morning in their hotel room Theda and Hunter were dressed in stone-washed jeans, sweaters and light coats ready to go out and have breakfast at Dooky Chase's restaurant.

"Um-m-m. Got my mouth set for shrimp omelet and wild plum jam," Theda told him, kissing the tip of his nose.

Hunter laughed. "Now, don't start the touchy-feely games or we'll never get out of here."

Theda grinned. "What'd I do? I love you and I just can't help showing it. Hey, you're a fine slab of meat, Mr. Davis. Can I help it if you keep me turned on?"

"Yeah, well…" he began, and his cell phone rang. After a minute Theda watched with alarm as shock traversed his face and she heard him breathe hard and ask questions of "When?" and "Where?"

After a few minutes he stood numbly holding the phone.

"Honey, what is it?"

"It's Curt. He's been in an accident and they say he may not live. We have to go at once."

She heard herself murmur, "Oh, Lord, be with us now!"

The next hours passed in a blur as she managed a lucky flight out early that afternoon. It was pre-Carnival time and more people were coming in than were going out. When they had a brief lull between packing and making calls, she asked him what the person calling him had said.

"A social worker at the hospital said they brought Curt in at three this morning. Why weren't we called then? God, I won't ask questions. Please, just let him *live*."

That night at the Richmond hospital, they found Curt's room. He lay swathed in bandages, moaning softly. "Curt," Hunter called softly. There was no response.

His doctor was there with a nurse. Hunter identified Theda and himself and the doctor's face lit up. "Boy, am I glad you're here. He's unconscious and has been since he was brought in."

Hunter waited impatiently for the doctor to finish before he asked, "How is he doing now? The call to us said he may..." He was going to say "may not live," but he couldn't get it out. This couldn't be! This was the nightmare of his life.

The doctor nodded, understanding what Hunter wanted to say. "He's not out of the woods. We've operated. It was a terrible wound. A piece of metal pierced his chest, going too near his heart and there's internal bleeding. We're fighting as hard as we can."

Theda caught Hunter's hand and held it tightly as angry tears ran down his face. Then he drew on all his courage and brushed the tears away. His only living son might die. The weight of it seemed more than he could bear.

The doctor was speaking and it was a few seconds before Hunter could focus. "I need to talk with you," the doctor said. "There are some things I've got to know about Curt that will help us. Will you go with me?"

"She'll come with us," Hunter said, nodding toward Theda.

"Of course. Curt's in shock, Mr. Davis," the doctor said. "He'll need your love and support if he's going to make it through this."

Later Hunter sat by Curt's bedside and studied the long, finely molded head of his son as he never had before.

"Dad," came the hoarse whisper.

Hunter caught his hand and held it tightly. "I'm right here, son. I'll always be here for you. *Always*."

There was a barely perceptible fluttering of Curt's lids and Hunter couldn't be certain he saw it. He pressed his hand again.

"Dad." This time the voice was a bit stronger.

"Yes, Curt. It's Dad and I'm here. I'll always be here." He squeezed Curt's hand, stroked it, held it to his lips. "Dear God, I love you so much. You have to live, boy. You've got to stay with me."

The monitors were all around and the nurse was there much of the time. When he could tear his eyes from Curt, Hunter glanced at the monitors and saw their steady green wave lines.

Hunter talked to Curt with his deepest heart. He sat there for hours. All the while, Hunter talked to Curt and he would have sworn Curt could hear him.

Chapter 23

Hunter and Theda sat in a waiting area near Curt's room the next morning.

Around Curt Hunter tried to be upbeat, but his heart had been hurt with savage cruelty. The doctor had said that Curt was much improved, but there was still internal bleeding.

"It's his *emotional* health I'm worried about," the doctor had said. "In his sleep he keeps telling his mother to stay away from him. If we could settle that…" He'd suddenly looked up with a deep frown. "You *will* be certain she doesn't see him. I hate to think what would happen if she does."

Hunter's eyes had narrowed to slits. "I'll see that that doesn't happen."

Both Theda and he sat lost in thought when the softly uncertain voice came from the doorway. "Hunter."

Hunter's head jerked up. A disheveled Helena stood just inside the door. "How *is* he?"

"Not good," he said brusquely. "You can't see him, Helena, and you can't stay. Doctor's orders and mine."

"And with good reason." She came forward. "I have to talk to you."

"I have nothing to say to you."

Standing, with her legs shaking, she told him. "It was all a lie, Hunter. There was never a hysterectomy. I mean, I never had a hysterectomy."

"*What?* What in the hell are you talking about? You said…"

"I know what I said. May I sit down?"

"For a minute, but you can't stay. I'm not going to risk Curt's life by letting you stay, or letting you see him."

"It's all right. I know this is my fault and I'm sorry and I know that doesn't help. My whole miserable life came before me when I heard about his accident. Why couldn't it have been me?"

"It wasn't you, though, was it?" Hunter said bitterly.

"At least you know now you have nothing to feel guilty about. I knew I couldn't hold Carl, but I wanted my share of what I could get from him and I left you and Curt. He refused to let Curt even visit, after promising me before we were married that he could stay with us. I wasn't married a week before I knew I'd made a horrible mistake and I wanted to come back to you. But that's water over the dam.

"I set up the photo deal with Keatha and I had a lover, even as I begged Curt to help us get together again as a family. And then, Curt saw me and my lover…"

A dry sob escaped her throat. "I have so much to answer for."

"Yes, you have," Hunter said, still trying to digest the information she had given him about her hysterectomy being a lie. He caught Theda's hand and gripped it tightly.

And Theda felt shock waves go through her as she realized she had felt this all along. For long moments she had to struggle for breath.

All three were silent until Helena said, "I won't ask you to forgive me, but I had to let you know. Now you and Curt are lost to me forever and I deserve to be alone…."

When he could breathe again, Hunter reflected that he had caused her pain with the accident and he was very sorry for that, but not the lifelong pain he'd flayed himself alive for causing. But the pain in his heart over Curt was so deep, it left no room for rejoicing about anything else.

"How did you know about Curt?" he asked her.

"Keatha was at Harney and she overheard Andre Lord and Angela Smith talking about it. She asked questions and demanded answers from Andre."

She looked at him with haunted eyes and she said again, "I won't ask you or Theda to forgive me. You couldn't possibly, but I had to tell you. I'll go now…."

"Helena," Hunter said.

"Yes?" She looked up hopefully.

"Don't try to see him in any way. Don't go near his room. Don't contact him at all. Do you understand?"

She nodded dully. "I understand and I'll stay

away from him. That's the least I can do. *Oh, God, I'm so sorry!*" Her voice broke on a dry sob.

"You could never be sorry enough. I think it's best you leave now."

She got up then and began to walk slowly from the room, but she stopped and looked back. "I'll be moving back to Texarkana as soon as I can get some things together. Keatha will ship the rest. Please let me call you to see how Curt is…."

Tears blinded her then as she waited for an answer. "Very well," Hunter said. "Give me your cell-phone number and I'll call you."

She gave him the number, and he committed it to memory. She left then, wanting to look back, but not daring to lest she antagonize Hunter and he not call her at all. The doctor came into the room, excitement in his voice and stance. He glanced at Helena, surmising who she was.

"He's made a significant upturn," the doctor said to Hunter. "He's calling for you."

As Hunter sprang up, he brushed past Helena and she breathed faster with joy. Maybe it would be all right then. Maybe God wouldn't punish her by taking Curt.

Going up the hall, the doctor told them, "He's

much more functional than we thought he'd be at this point. He's murmuring a little and I'm allowing it, but don't talk too much and I'll be there to see that he doesn't talk too much."

Curt smiled weakly as they came into the room. He said, "Hello, Dad, Dr. Coles," in a hoarse voice before they could reach him. At his side, Hunter took his hand. "Hey, you're looking like you could be getting game."

The boy smiled a little. "Want—to tell—you— something."

"Okay," the doctor said, "but not too much talk."

"All right. Dad, I heard you tell me to come back. I wanted to leave but I couldn't. I came back. I love you both."

The effort was tiring him and the doctor said gently, "We have to stop for now. You're doing so much better. You'll be talking all you want to very shortly."

"Okay," Curt said, and stopped talking, but he smiled again and pressed his father's hand with more strength than Hunter would have thought he had.

Curt fell asleep then and leaving the room Hunter felt tears of joy flood his heart. Out in the hall, he took Theda's hand. "Let's go to that big window at the end of the hall, let the sunlight pour in, and we'll pray."

It was as the doctor predicted. Curt began to heal very quickly and at the end of two more days he was taking some steps. Hunter and Theda came into his room on the third day as Curt's lunch tray was being taken out. He patted his stomach. "Hey, hospital food's not so bad. Wouldn't want to eat it too long, though."

Both Hunter and Theda kissed him on the cheek and he grinned, then got somber. "Dad, I want to thank you. I might not have made it without you."

"But you *did* make it and I'll never stop thanking God."

"Yeah." He cleared his throat. "Dad, I've been thinking about what you told me back when my best buddy broke my finger in a fight…."

"Yes."

"I'm going to forgive Mom. I can't forget what she did. I just can't, but remember what you told me?"

Hunter smiled. "I remember, but suppose you tell me."

"You said when you don't forgive, the other

person owns your body and soul." He smiled a little bitterly then. "I'm too mad with Mom to have her owning me, so I'll forgive her, but I don't want to see her for a while."

"She's going back to Texarkana soon, son. I tell her every day how you're doing. She's been here. The doctor and I said she couldn't see you."

"Thanks, Dad. Some things hurt, but when I'm all the way grown-up, maybe I'll understand."

Hunter expelled a harsh sigh. "Being grown-up is no excuse for certain behavior. I'm sure you'll do just fine when you're grown-up." He smiled then. "Didn't I train you?"

"Yeah. And Dr. Coles, I'm sorry I was mean to you. Please forgive me."

"Oh, Curt, of course. You were just mixed-up. I can understand that."

Curt took a deep breath and grinned. "Now, you want to know what I want?"

Both people said they did and Curt's face was suddenly wreathed in smiles. "I want you two to get married, and you don't wait until I'm well. Then, what's wrong with a second ceremony with me as best man?"

Theda and Hunter looked at each other, happy and astonished.

Curt's eyes crinkled with laughter. "Now, that's not a suggestion, it's an order!"

"Sounds good to me," Hunter told him. "I want to wait a few days, though, until you're even better and you're up and around. Then we'll do it. How's that for following orders?"

"Great!"

Hunter took Theda's hand and held it, looking deeply into her eyes as Curt gazed lovingly at them both. Hunter kissed that hand and told her, "I will *never* be without you again."

Theda nodded, too full with joy to speak.

Epilogue

"I now pronounce you man and wife. You may kiss the bride."

At sunrise, three days after Curt had ordered that they be married, Hunter and Theda stood before a justice of the peace in Elkins, Maryland, and heard the blessed words. Hunter intended to kiss her lightly and let go, but the kiss caught fire and deepened, filling her heart with joy. The justice of the peace cleared his throat softly and both looked up and caught his eye. The man was smiling broadly thinking they were certainly off to a good start.

The wife of the justice of the peace, a small gray-haired woman with twinkling eyes, stood as witness. Theda's off-white silk faille suit was plain and flattered her glowing cinnamon skin. She wore a small, fitted off-white hat with a veil that came to her eyebrows, and carried a bouquet of white baby cattleya orchids. Hunter had placed the yellow diamond and platinum wedding band on her finger to match the ring he had given her in the Poconos. Now he couldn't take his eyes from her face and form and he hotly fantasized about the time that lay before them.

Curt was healing swiftly and would leave the hospital within the week, but he would not hear of them waiting to be married. The doctors felt the boy would continue to heal completely from his injuries. Curt was almost his old self again, still teasing Hunter about getting him a Hog.

Hunter had kept in touch with Helena, who stayed with a friend in Dallas in order to work daily with a psychiatrist. Theda still shuddered when she thought of how close this woman had come to destroying her. It had almost cost Curt his life to bring Helena to her senses.

A gorgeous sunrise lay on the horizon. They faced a bank of floor-to-ceiling windows that caught the sun's fire and radiance. Theda thought she had seldom seen anything so glorious—she smiled mischievously—except Hunter's joyful face as he kept kissing her with his eyes.

Hunter touched her face and whispered, "I've said it so often, but I can never say it enough. I will never be without you again."

And she echoed his words with tears of ecstasy, making her eyes shine like stars.

Trouble was her middle name...his was danger!

Elaine OVERTON

His Holiday Bride

Fleeing from a dangerous pursuer, Amber Lockhart takes refuge in the home—and arms—of Paul Gutierrez. But the threat posed by the man who's after her doesn't compare with the peril to Amber's heart from her sexy Latin protector.

THE LOCKHARTS

THREE WEDDINGS AND A REUNION
FOR FOUR SASSY SISTERS, ROMANCE CHANGES EVERYTHING!

Available the first week of October wherever books are sold.

KIMANI™
ROMANCE

www.kimanipress.com

KPE00361007

No commitment, no strings, no promises...
but then love got in the way!

LET ME
Love *You*

LINDA WALTERS

Skye Thompson's Miami getaway brought more than
sun, sand and warm breezes...it led to steamy passion
with Dr. Terrance Marshall. Their weekend together
was just what a woman on the rebound needed—until
the unwanted complication of love interfered. But with
both living separate, busy lives in different cities, could
Skye and Terrance find a way to be together?

Available the first week of October
wherever books are sold.

He looked good enough to eat...and she was hungry!

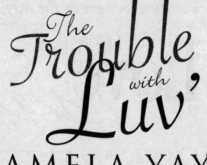

The Trouble with Luv'

PAMELA YAYE

When feisty, aggressive, sensuous Ebony Garrett
propositions him, Xavier Reed turns her down cold.
He's more interested in demure, classy, marriage-
minded women. But when a church function reveals
Ebony's softer side, Xavier melts like butter.
Only, is he really ready to risk the heat?

"Yaye has written a beautiful romance
with a lot of sensual heat."
—*Imani Book Club Review* on *Other People's Business*

*Available the first week of October
wherever books are sold.*

KIMANI™
ROMANCE

www.kimanipress.com KPPY0391007

National bestselling author

ROCHELLE ALERS

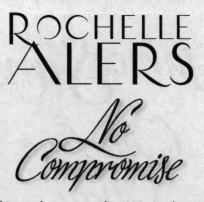

No Compromise

In charge of a program for victimized women, Jolene Walker has no time or energy for a personal life...until she meets army captain Michael Kirkland. This sexy, compelling man is tempting her to trade her long eighteen-hour workdays for sultry nights of sizzling passion. But their bliss is shattered when Jolene takes on a mysterious new client, plunging her into a world of terrifying danger.

"Alers paints such vivid descriptions that when Jolene becomes the target of a murderer, you almost feel as though someone you know is in great danger."
—*Library Journal*

Available the first week of October
wherever books are sold.

ARABESQUE®

www.kimanipress.com

KPRA0181007

Will one secret destroy their love?

Award-winning author

Janice Sims

One fine Day

The Bryant Family trilogy continues with this heartfelt story in which Jason Bryant tries to convince lovely bookstore owner Sara Minton to marry him. Their love is unlike anything Jason has ever felt, and he knows Sara feels the same way...so why does she keep refusing him, saying she'll marry him "one day"? He knows she's hiding something...but what?

Available the first week of October
wherever books are sold.

ARABESQUE®

www.kimanipress.com

KPJS0141007

*I*t happened in an instant.
One stormy December night, two cars collided,
shattering four peoples' lives forever....

Essence Bestselling Author

MONICA MCKAYHAN

The EVENING After

In the aftermath of the accident that took her husband,
Lainey Williams struggles with loss, guilt and regret over her
far-from-perfect union. Nathan Sullivan, on the other hand, is
dealing with a comatose wife, forcing him to reassess his life.

It begins as two grieving people offering comfort and
friendship to one another. But as trust...and passion...
grow, a secret is revealed, risking the newly rebuilt
lives of these two people.

The Evening After is "another wonderful novel
that will leave you satisfied and uplifted."
—Margaret Johnson-Hudge, author of *True Lies*

*Available the first week of October
wherever books are sold.*

sepia™

www.kimanipress.com   KPMM0371007

GET THE GENUINE LOVE
YOU DESERVE...

NATIONAL BESTSELLING AUTHOR

Vikki Johnson

Addicted to
COUNTERFEIT
LOVE

Many people in today's world are unable to recognize
what a genuine loving partnership should be and
often sabotage one when it does come along. In this
moving volume, Vikki Johnson offers memorable
words that will help readers identify destructive love
patterns and encourage them to demand the love
that they are entitled to.

Available the first week of October wherever books are sold.

www.kimanipress.com　　KPVJ0381007